catch me if I fall

Also by Barry Jonsberg

A Song Only I Can Hear
Game Theory
Pandora Jones (Book 1) Admission
Pandora Jones (Book 2) Deception
Pandora Jones (Book 3) Reckoning
My Life as an Alphabet
Being Here
Cassie
Ironbark
Dreamrider
It's Not All About YOU, Calma!
The Whole Business with Kiffo and the Pitbull

BARRY JONSBERG

catch me
if I fall

ALLEN&UNWIN
SYDNEY·MELBOURNE·AUCKLAND·LONDON

This project has been assisted by the Australian Government through the Australia Council, its arts funding and advisory body

First published by Allen & Unwin in 2020

Allen & Unwin
83 Alexander Street
Crows Nest NSW 2065
Australia
Phone: (61 2) 8425 0100
Email: info@allenandunwin.com
Web: www.allenandunwin.com

 A catalogue record for this book is available from the National Library of Australia

ISBN 978 1 76087 761 3

For teaching resources, explore www.allenandunwin.com/resources/for-teachers

Cover & text design by Debra Billson
Cover illustration by Iaroslava Daragan/Shutterstock
Set in 11/16 pt Sabon by Midland Typesetters
Printed in Australia in September 2020 by McPherson's Printing Group

10 9 8 7 6 5 4 3 2 1

For Evelyn Rose Lutz, with love from Bampa

SIX YEARS AGO

The storm had taken out the power again, so Aiden and I were in our beds and Mum was reading us a story by candlelight. I remember thinking that stories were so much better by candlelight because the flame danced and that sent ripples of shadows and light across Mum's face as she read. It's like her moving face was part of the story, that the words changed her expression as if they touched a switch inside her, turned something on and off, on and off.

Aiden had the bedcovers up to his eyes, which were wide, unblinking and fixed on Mum. The candlelight made his hair, black and wavy like mine, shiver against the white of the pillowcase. It's as if there were thin worms crawling and creeping across his scalp and the thought made me giggle and then it made me afraid.

I don't know what the story was about because I'd been thinking about candles and lights and worms, but Aiden was drinking it in, thirsty for every word.

Mum closed the book and we cried out together.

'Another one! Please?'

But she wouldn't tell us another one, no matter how hard we begged. We needed to get to sleep. We had school in the morning (though without electricity, we all knew that wasn't going to happen). We couldn't bully her. We only ever got one story at bedtime because … *that's the way it was*. Nighty night. Don't let the bed bugs bite. But we argued anyway. Because … *that's the way it was*.

'Can we keep the candle in here, please?'

Aiden was scared of the dark. I wasn't, because I was tougher than him. I'm the oldest. By three minutes, Mum said, but that explained a lot. It explained why I'm always the one who makes decisions, why I'm the one in charge. Aiden never argued about this because it's a fact and facts don't care if you argue with them and they won't change simply because you don't like them.

Aiden was quite smart, though.

'Ashleigh, tell your brother why you can't have the candle in here,' said Mum.

I sat up in bed and took a deep breath.

'Because it's dangerous,' I said. 'If one of us – probably Aiden because he can be quite clumsy – if one of us knocks over the candle in the night, then we could set the beds on fire and burn the house down and burn all of us to death so that's why we can only have electric night-lights but we can't have those because there isn't any power because of the storm and we've run out of batteries.'

I had to take another deep breath then because all those words had ridden on the wave of my last one and my lungs were empty. Mum smiled.

'A good answer, Ashleigh,' she said. I beamed. 'If a little self-satisfied.' I didn't know what she meant by that, but thought it was probably good. She turned to Aiden and smoothed his bedsheets. 'So one of you – maybe even Ashleigh, difficult though it might be for anyone to believe – could have an accident. We have to keep you safe, my babies.' He nodded, just as another clap of thunder sounded nearby. It made the glass of water on my bedside shake. It was a little bit funny, as if nodding his head made the thunder happen.

'Anyway, if this storm keeps up, you won't need any light,' Mum said. 'You'll have more than enough of the natural variety. Think you'll be able to sleep through it, kiddlypunks?'

We all knew the storm would go on for hours and hours and we probably wouldn't have electricity to cook breakfast in the morning. That's the way it normally worked. And we also knew the thunder wouldn't stop us sleeping. We'd slept through cyclones and this was nothing compared to that.

'Yes, Mamma,' said Aiden.

'Of course,' I said.

Mum sat on my bed again, which was a bit strange and definitely not part of the routine.

'I think you're old enough to hear this,' Mum said, 'so I want you to pay close attention.'

We both sat up in bed. Was this going to be another story, despite what she said? Whatever it was, it was exciting.

'You are identical twins,' she said. We knew that. Of course we knew that. It made us rare and extremely special. We didn't say anything, though. Just waited. 'Brother and sister,' she continued, 'with an unbreakable bond between you. It's a marvellous thing. A most marvellous thing.'

I swallowed a yawn. I was tired and this wasn't very interesting or exciting after all. Well, so far. Of course we were special. I'd always known that.

'But it also means you have responsibilities towards each other,' she said. 'Responsibilities means having sometimes to do things you might not want to do to help and protect the other. Do you know what I mean?'

We both nodded, but I'm not sure either of us quite got it. Maybe that was why Mum gave an example.

'Let's say I did leave the candle in here and Ashleigh knocked it over in the night…' I opened my mouth to protest, but Mum held up a hand in the stop position, so I did. 'And you woke, Aiden, to the bedroom on fire. What's the first thing you'd do?'

'I'd wake Ashleigh and get her out of the bedroom.'

'Yes. Good. Why?'

'Because she's my sister and I have to protect her.'

Mum beamed, leaned over and stroked Aiden's cheek. A stab of jealousy made me flinch. I could have answered that question. That small sliver of affection was rightfully mine and I felt the pain of its absence.

'That's what being brother and sister means,' she said. 'It's what family means. There's an old saying, children. Siblings are there to catch you when you fall. If something goes wrong – and it doesn't have to be something big, like a fire; it could be just one of you feeling sad, or having a bit of a bad time – then the other should always be there to help. Always! That's what I mean about responsibilities. You, Aiden, must always be there to catch Ashleigh if she falls.' He nodded.

'And I'll catch Aiden,' I said. 'He's falling all the time.' *That's because he's so clumsy*, I thought, but I didn't say it out loud.

'Yes,' said Mum. 'You must promise me that you'll always look after each other.'

We made that promise with all of a six-year-old's solemnity. Later, after Mum had blown out the candle and left us to our sleep, Aiden's hand reached across the darkness between our beds and took mine. He could be *so* childish, like when he called Mum, Mamma.

We fell asleep holding hands, the lightning flashing silver and black and the thunder playing drumrolls on the bedroom window.

present day ...

1

Aiden tried to hold my hand, but I was too old for that. So was he, obviously. I kicked him gently in the foot and he let go, but not before everyone must have seen. Just what I needed on our first day. I wiped the hand he'd held on my dress and clasped both hands behind my back. My face burned and the more I thought about it burning, the hotter it got. Great. Just great.

Mr Meredith stood behind us and placed one hand on my shoulder and one on Aiden's.

'How lucky are we, class?' he said over the tops of our heads. No one said anything, but then I guess it *was* a question that didn't need an answer. 'We don't just have one student joining us today, but two.'

The class gazed at us. It would be good to report that they weren't too interested, that they were staring out of windows or picking at fingernails, but the simple truth is they were staring at us like we were from another planet.

The temperature of my face ratcheted up another couple of degrees.

'Not only that,' continued Mr Meredith, 'but they are *identical* twins.' There was wonder in his voice as if we were all witnessing a miracle. 'Who can tell me about identical twins?'

A girl in the front row put her hand up, but Mr Meredith ignored her. I guessed she always put her hand up, the class know-it-all who made everyone else feel small. I'd seen old movies where this happened. A boy towards the back raised his arm, but it was slow and unsure in its journey. Mr Meredith took his hand from my shoulder and it appeared in front of my eyes, index finger pointing.

'Yes, Daniel,' he said.

'Two children born from the same mother who look like each other,' he said, but his voice was cracking and unsure. There was silence and it was obvious he was expected to say something else. 'At the same time,' he added.

'Very good, Daniel,' said Mr Meredith. 'Excellent.'

The girl at the front still had her hand up. Mr Meredith's sigh played across my cheek.

'Yes, Charlotte?' he said.

Charlotte sat up straighter, jiggled her shoulders as if making sure they both lined up correctly.

'Please sir,' she said. 'Identical twins are from one zygote, which splits and forms two embryos, which means that these two can't be identical twins because you can't have identical twins of the opposite gender. So they must be fraternal twins who come from two separate eggs fertilised separately.'

There was a sprinkle of laughter. I guessed it was at the mention of eggs. Charlotte spun in her chair, anger on her face.

'It's true,' she said. She swung back towards us. 'Isn't it, sir? I'm right, aren't I, sir? Tell them.'

'Indeed you are, Charlotte. Perfectly correct.' The teacher moved in front of us and clasped his hands together. 'I imagine the laughter came from the mention of eggs. Hard-boiled, fried, scrambled, yes? Delicious on toast. But Charlotte is, as always, right. We all came from eggs, children. But this doesn't make us chickens, does it? Do anyone of us really feel the urge to do this?'

He crouched down, knuckles on each hand touching, elbows wide. He strutted in front of the class, elbows pumping, head jerking backwards and forwards, clucking and clucking. The class groaned at first but then laughed harder and harder as he turned in front of them. I felt a smile on my lips. This teacher was either going to be the best or really annoying. It was early days so I only smiled.

He straightened up.

'Well, *I* felt the urge, obviously, but that's just me, children. When I am on yard duty outside and watch you play, I see running, I see jumping, I see skipping. But I definitely do not see chicken impersonations.' He paused. 'At least, not yet.' Mr Meredith turned towards us and spread his arms wide. 'But I am being very rude to our guests who almost certainly want to get out of the spotlight. Please welcome two new members of the class. This is Ashleigh Delatour and her twin brother Aiden Delatour. Can I hear how lucky are we, children?'

Everyone clapped, which made my face go redder. I glanced over at Aiden, but his face was emotionless, as always.

'Would you like to sit together?' Mr Meredith bent and whispered to us when the applause had died down.

'No, thank you,' I said. 'We are quite independent.' I was trying to be confident, but my voice was a little shaky. The teacher nodded.

'Then pick a place,' he said. 'Anywhere you like.'

I looked around the room, but it wasn't a difficult decision. I was desperately in need of a friend and it seemed obvious that the girl at the front, Charlotte, was probably in the same boat. Know-it-alls, I thought, would be left alone during playtime on the grounds that you got your fill of them in class. Plus, it was a good strategy to sit towards the front. Not only did it allow you to hear everything better, but those at the back, from what I'd read on the subject, often got a reputation. Not a very good reputation. Charlotte beamed at me as I sat down, but I placed my hands carefully on the desk and looked straight ahead.

Aiden, it turned out, sat at the back.

'Mr Meredith can be a bit of a spoilsport at times.'

Charlotte and I sat on the school verandah, under a huge fan. Mr Meredith had checked his tablet coming up to lunchtime and told us we couldn't go out to play because the UV levels were dangerous. This was no surprise. The UV levels were *always* dangerous. The class had groaned and offered to wear extra sunblock and legionnaire caps, but he still wouldn't let us.

'And a chicken,' I pointed out.

Charlotte laughed.

'Yes. He does that kind of stuff all the time. He's funny. You know, with some teachers it would be like he's trying too hard to be funny, but he's … I don't know. He's genuine. He *likes* kids. And there are too many teachers who seem to hate us.'

This was true, but I hadn't really thought about it until Charlotte said it. Quite a few of my old teachers had obviously not liked kids at all, judging by the way they treated us, even in distance learning when we were all hundreds of kilometres away from each other. I wondered why they'd gone into teaching in the first place. It'd be like a farmer who doesn't like animals or crops, or a doctor who doesn't like medicine.

'Why's your brother sitting by himself?'

I glanced over at Aiden. He was about ten metres away and he was alone because everyone else was as close as possible to the fans. He doesn't seem to care about the heat. He just sweats and mops his face with a handkerchief. Sometimes, when we go for a walk around

13

our garden, he gets big circles of sweat under his armpits. That's more than a little gross.

'He's a bit of a loner,' I said.

I didn't tell her that he was under strict instructions to keep his distance while we were in school. Everyone thinks that just because we're twins we've got this kind of crazy bond between us. I mean, we do. We do *have* a bond. But it's not one that means we have to spend every second of our lives together, despite the fact that Aiden would be happy if we did. He's needy. Me too, I suppose. But the difference is I need my own space and I need my own friends. It's Aiden's problem if he can live without either.

'I'd love to have a twin brother,' said Charlotte. 'It's horrible being an only child.'

Everyone said this and I'd learned not to argue. I didn't tell them that they didn't have to share parents' affection or that sometimes being by yourself was a kind of heaven, that if they knew the problems they probably wouldn't be so keen to grow up with someone who looks just like you and has similar ways of thinking and speaking. Having said that, I'm a different personality to Aiden. Totally different. He's quiet and he's always considerate of my feelings. I'm not so quiet, though I *am* considerate of my feelings. I told him that once but he didn't get the joke.

'Yeah,' I said. 'It's cool. But we *are* identical, you know.'

Charlotte shook her head.

'You may look very similar, but you can't be identical. Trust me. I know about these things.'

Dad personally picked us up from school. Mum was away in Melbourne at a business conference. She's often away, which is a bummer in one way but good in another. Dad is a much better cook than Mum and he doesn't mind baking chips. Mum is very anti chips. In fact, she's anti everything except vegetables, which we grow in our vegetable plots behind the house. I've pointed out that chips *are* vegetables, but it makes no difference because she thinks veggies have to be green (with a few exceptions, not including chips). I don't *mind* green vegetables, but I'll have them fried given half the chance. Aiden doesn't care one way or the other, since he doesn't eat anything. Well, he does, but it's not food as we know it.

Aiden and I went for a swim in our pool, while Dad made dinner. Vegetable frittata and chips, he said. One of my favourites.

I have to be honest. If there's one thing that Aiden is better at than me, it's swimming. He can go the whole length of the pool underwater and when he's really trying he can crush me at freestyle. I know this because I watched him once when he didn't know I was around and he was part-dolphin. There's no way I could come close to him. But when we have races, he always lets me win. By a little bit, as if he was really trying but just came up short. Sometimes I like that and sometimes it annoys me. Today we only did a few laps of lazy breaststroke.

'What did you think of school, Aiden?' I asked.

He shrugged and brushed wet hair from his face.

'It's okay,' he replied. 'I think Mr Meredith might be nice. You know, Ashleigh? *Really* nice.'

'Yeah,' I said. 'Silly in a way grown-ups normally aren't.'

'He likes his students.'

'That's what Charlotte said.'

'Is Charlotte going to be your friend?'

This time I shrugged.

'Maybe. It's early days.'

Suddenly, I didn't feel like talking, so I bobbed about on the edge of the pool and watched, through tinted windows, the hills in the distance. They were purple, patched with green and cottoned by heat haze. The early evening air swam. Aiden did laps, left me to my thoughts.

Dad quizzed us about school over dinner. The frittata was delicious and the chips were crisp and crunchy, so I ate them one nibble at a time, savouring their earthiness. I'd pulled those potatoes from the ground myself. Aiden left most of the talking to me, as always.

'Well,' said Dad. 'I'm glad the first day went well. The school has a great reputation and it wasn't easy to get you enrolled.'

I knew that. The fees were huge, though Mum and Dad could afford them.But they didn't take just anyone. I have no idea how difficult it was to get the school to accept us, but Mum and Dad had interview after interview, as well as dishing out plenty of money. When we lived in Queensland, we'd started with School of the Air tuition because the place we lived in was pretty much cut off from civilisation. Since moving to Sydney, though, we'd had tutors come to the house and that was okay in a way, but not okay in another way. I wanted to make friends with other girls and although Mum and Dad told me I was lucky I had a friend in my twin brother – and that plenty of people would be *very* envious of us for that – I made it clear that it wasn't enough. I love my brother, yeah. But he's not a friend. He's not someone I can share…well, girl things with. Obviously. This school will change all that. I think Charlotte will become a friend, but maybe others as well. It was my first day after all and I'd made a terrific start in the friends department.

Mum video-called us at bedtime from her hotel in Melbourne. She and Dad had a chat first and then he put us on when we were in bed reading.

'How was your first day at school, kiddlypunks?'

I wished, for the thousandth time, she'd stop calling us that. It's embarrassing.

'It was great, Mum,' I said. 'I think I made a friend already.'

We told her everything about the day, the classes and what we'd learned and especially about Mr Meredith. Mum smiled, nodded and told us she'd be back the day after tomorrow, assuming flights weren't disrupted, which was a big assumption. She told us she loved us and to make sure the bed bugs didn't bite and we told her we loved her and that there weren't any bed bugs and then we handed her back to Dad.

Aiden wanted to talk, but I wasn't in the mood. I thought it was crazy we still had to share a room when we were twelve years old. It wasn't like there weren't plenty of bedrooms in our new house, but Mum and Dad wouldn't hear of it. *You can look out for each other during the night*, they said. *We're asleep. Duh*, I pointed out. Didn't make a difference.

I switched off my bedside lamp and turned towards the wall, mainly to discourage Aiden from talking. He wouldn't say anything if he thought I was going to sleep. But I wasn't going to sleep just yet. I was going to go over in my head the entire day, relive every moment. And I knew that when I did fall asleep, I'd dream of school, Mr Meredith and Charlotte. It would be delicious.

Aiden doesn't dream. Or so he says. Maybe he doesn't remember them. That's equal parts weird and sad, if you ask me.

2

I knew it was a very bad idea. As soon as I had it, I knew. But I wouldn't listen, even to myself.

Mr Meredith checked his tablet again before lunch; this time the news was better and we were allowed to play outside, though only with hats and sunblock that he personally inspected. *Duty of care*, he muttered as he examined us. *You get skin cancer, I'm the one responsible*. Nobody but Mr Meredith seemed to worry about that. Some of the boys and a couple of the girls immediately rushed to the basketball court. Charlotte and I stayed under shade at a bench and opened our lunchboxes. I had an apple, sliced carrots and a boiled egg from our very own chook, Kentucky. Charlotte had a sandwich with what looked like beef in it. She noticed me staring.

'I love beef,' she said, taking a small bite. 'Don't you, Ashleigh?'

'Oh yeah,' I said. 'But Mum and Dad won't let me have any. They say it's "not sustainable".' I made the quotation marks in the air with my fingers. 'That's why I'm stuck with fruit and vegetables. Always vegetables. I get sick of it, to be honest.'

Charlotte put her sandwich back in her lunchbox. She'd only taken the one bite.

'Have you ever eaten mango?' she asked.

'Of course,' I replied. 'We lived in Queensland before moving to Sydney. There were mangoes all around us.'

'I *love* mango. Only had it once, but that taste...' She got this dreamy look in her eyes. 'Now there's a huge shortage and you can't get them anywhere. Except...'

'Except?'

'Someone told me there's a tree in Victoria Park, a few minutes from here. A couple of trees. And that there are mangoes growing on them.'

I laughed.

'They must've been joking. Mangoes don't grow in Sydney.'

Charlotte picked up her sandwich again, thought better of it and put it back.

'That used to be true,' she said. 'But climate change has altered all sorts of things. Most of it bad, but the occasional bit good. Apparently, Sydney's climate is now hot enough that mangoes *can* grow. Jessica, who's in the year above us, says she's seen them in Victoria Park. And trust me, Jessica knows what she's talking about.'

I chewed on a carrot stick. It seemed unlikely that Charlotte would make this up. A bit like yesterday with the zygote pronouncement, she'd shown her brilliance on almost everything today in class. Her head's stuffed with knowledge.

'Even if that's true,' I said. Charlotte gave me a sharp glance. 'And I'm sure it is,' I added. 'Then someone would have picked them by now. There's no way free fruit would last long in any park.'

Charlotte sighed.

'That's probably true,' she said. 'Probably.'

That's when I had the idea.

'I'll go and check it out for you,' I said.

'When?'

'Right now. Me and Aiden will go now. It's just down Albert Street and if we run we'll be back way before the start of afternoon classes.' I was excited. If there was a way to impress my new friend, make sure she saw me as someone worthy of friendship, then this was it. I got to my feet.

'The school won't let you out at lunchtime,' said Charlotte. 'It's a really firm rule because they need to know where you are at all times. You heard Mr Meredith and all that duty of care business. Anyway, it could be dangerous out there. You *know* there are parts of Sydney that are not … safe.'

I brushed aside her arguments, mainly because I was in that heady zone of imagination where the promise of success blinds you to fear. The way I thought about it was this – even if I *didn't* get a mango, and I was pretty sure they *couldn't* exist – I'd show her how I wasn't scared of anything, that I was a rebel, someone who acted on the spur of the moment without thinking of her own safety. I liked that vision of myself, even if it was a long way from the truth.

'We're fenced in,' Charlotte pointed out.

'It would take more than a fence to keep *me* in,' I said. 'Go talk to Mr Meredith. Distract him. Do a chicken impersonation. I'll be back soon.'

I ran to where Aidan was sitting, watching the basketball. He's good at most sports, but he wouldn't play unless I was on court with him. It's no wonder I always have to take the initiative.

'Come with me, Aiden,' I said and he didn't hesitate. It was like he was waiting for instruction.

'Where are we going?'

'Over the fence,' I said. 'And then to Victoria Park.'

'Why?'

'I'll explain as we go.'

To be fair to Aiden, he doesn't waste time arguing. When I put the toe of my school shoe into the chain link fence and climbed the two metres to its top, he was right there beside me. We dropped down onto the ground and scurried behind a straggly bush maybe fifty metres away. I brushed hair from my eyes and peered from our hiding space. As far as I could tell, no one in the school had noticed us. No alarm had been raised. I squatted down on my haunches and tried to regulate my breathing.

Now I had time to think, I wondered what the hell I was doing. There wouldn't be a mango tree. That was just crazy. And Charlotte was right about one thing – there *were* dangerous places round here. Mum and Dad had told us stories about the horrible things that could happen to people who wandered off by themselves. What had seemed like a good idea – proving my courage and worth – now seemed stupid and pointless. But I couldn't just climb back in. Charlotte would know I'd got cold feet and I couldn't face that. It crossed my mind to just wait there for ten or fifteen minutes, hidden from view, and then go back, tell Charlotte I couldn't find the tree. Or maybe that I *had* found it but someone must have beaten me to it and taken the fruit. Aiden would back me up.

But somehow I couldn't bring myself to do that either. The park could only be a minute or two down the street; in fact, when I glanced over my shoulder I caught a glimpse of trees just a few hundred metres away. We could be there and back in no time at all.

'Come on, Aiden,' I said.

I tried explaining as we walked, but it was difficult to find the right words. For one thing, confessing that I was doing this purely to impress Charlotte would make me look like an idiot, and even though I didn't care too much what Aiden thought, I drew the line at that. So I told him that I'd heard there were mangoes growing in the park and that I needed to check it out for myself. All brave, resourceful and independent. I have no idea if he believed me.

'This is dangerous, Ash,' he said. 'If Mum and Dad find out…'

'Then we'd better be careful they *don't* find out, okay?' I replied. He didn't say anything to that but I could tell from the way he kept glancing all around as we walked that he was on high alert for any threat. And I have to confess that the further we walked the more scared I became. It was a strange world out there – an unfamiliar world, by and large – and apprehension was like hot breath on the back of my neck. The smallest sound made me jump and my skin felt hyper-sensitive.

'Calm down,' I said to Aiden. 'You're making me nervous.'

He didn't say anything.

We arrived at the end of Albert Street and the park was laid out before us across the road. There was a slightly strange stone arch in cream, maroon and pale blue and I could make out an inscription across it that read *Richard Hellyer Memorial Entrance*. The park itself was lush, though the grass obviously hadn't been cut in a long time. There'd been a number of storms recently and everywhere was green. Everywhere was also quiet. No traffic and, as far as I could see, no people in the park itself. My pulse steadied and I thought that maybe we should return now. I could mention the strangely named entrance as evidence I'd been and simply tell Charlotte that there were no mangoes. I'd shrug, apologise. Hey, no big deal. I tried, you know? But the quietness of the place made me want to at least set foot in the park. Just a small walk and then we'd go back. This was an adventure and I never had adventures.

Aiden held my hand as we crossed the road and this time I let him. We stopped in front of the entrance arch and I wondered what it was doing there. I mean, it wasn't an entrance as such. There was no fence or railings around the park, so you could just walk in anywhere you wanted. I couldn't see the point of it. Anyway, we walked through regardless – it seemed rude not to, since someone had obviously gone to the trouble of building it. We stopped just inside the park. The concrete path beneath our feet was cracked, with tufts of grass and weeds spreading across it, like nature was fighting to take it back.

It wasn't a great park, as parks go. No waterfalls, like I'd seen on videos, but I guess that wasn't surprising. No useful markers telling you the Latin names of the trees. Just grass and a few huge trees that I was pretty sure were Moreton Bay figs – I recognised them from when I lived in Queensland. No mango trees, that's for sure, though I supposed I couldn't know for certain unless I explored the entire place and I wasn't going to do that. I was on the point of telling Aiden that we should go back when I heard a noise behind us. We spun around.

A girl. She must have been sitting against the entrance post and we'd walked right past her. Now she got to her feet and I understood the noise that had brought her to our attention. She had a canister in her right hand and she was shaking it, twisting her wrist as if to mix the contents. She stood, legs splayed, shaking the can and staring at us.

Aiden stepped in front of me. She didn't seem like much of a threat, but Aiden never takes chances.

She was dirty, this girl. Her face had faint streaks of grime, especially under her eyes, which were such a bright green they seemed to pin you to the spot. Her legs were dirty as well, though the fluorescent yellow Nike trainers she wore were spotless. Shorts and a T-shirt, both ragged. She must have been around thirteen or fourteen; it was difficult to tell. Hair was cut short and uneven, like she'd done it herself without the help of a mirror. Her mouth was wide, nose a snub. But it was her eyes that held you. There was silence for ten or twelve beats.

'Hello,' I said. 'We don't mean you any harm.'

She didn't say anything, nor did her eyes stray from ours. She just carried on shaking the can. I started to get a little uneasy. Street kids could be dangerous, we'd been told, though there was scarcely anything of her, her build was so slight. It looked like a strong breeze would knock her over.

'We're leaving now,' I said and took a step towards her.

Immediately, she stopped shaking the can and a series of sounds behind us made us turn. Seven or eight kids dropped from the branches of the nearest fig tree, like strange and alien fruit. They landed elegantly, flexing their legs. Not one stumbled. Aiden stepped in front of me again, obviously – and reasonably – judging the threat to be greater on that side. My throat was dry as the kids walked towards us. Five boys and two girls, all ragged, dirty and tough-looking. I thought briefly about running, but there was no point. It was obvious they'd run us down in less than ten metres. We didn't have anything valuable, so there was no point trying to rob us. Then again, they might just decide to hurt us because … well, because we were different and maybe they were bored. I saw Aiden bunch his hands into fists.

They formed a rough circle and looked us up and down. The first girl moved into the circle. She'd started shaking the can again.

'We don't have anything of value,' I said. 'We're just a couple of schoolkids and we need to get back. I'm sorry if this is your place. We didn't know and we certainly didn't mean to trespass. We'd like to go now, if that's all right.'

Silence.

'Please,' I added.

'*Please*,' said the girl. She smiled, revealing a set of small, brilliantly white teeth. 'How very polite. Please. Thank you. After you. Don't mind if I do. Much appreciated.' She stopped smiling.

'We have nothing you want,' I said into the following silence.

'Oh, I dunno 'bout that,' said the girl. She took a step towards us, ignoring Aiden's attempt to block her. 'Those clothes look good to me. Better than mine anyway. Maybe we'll strip you naked, leave you 'ere to find your way home. If I'm feeling very generous, then you can wear my gear, but I dare say it wouldn't suit. Fleas, you know. Nasty. Definitely not your … *style*.'

'We'll call security,' said Aiden. That made most of them laugh.

'Ooooh,' said a boy. 'Not security! I'm scared, Xena. Protect me, Xena. Those bad, bad security officers.'

The girl held up the can and sprayed a fine black mist in front of our eyes. Aiden and I both took a step back.

'Or maybe I'll tag your bodies. That'd be cool. Xena's tag on your bare butts. You could show them to security. I'm a bit bored with marking out our territory, to be honest.' She pointed to the park entrance. On one of the pillars there was a large X in black spray paint and a smaller squiggle next to it that I couldn't make out. 'I need to branch out, develop my art,' she continued. 'What better than a couple of rich kids as my canvas?'

I started to cry then. I tried not to because I didn't think showing weakness was going to help us any, but I couldn't help it. Aiden's muscles were tensing. He was on the verge of attacking, I knew. He'd throw himself at the nearest boy and start punching. It wouldn't matter that he was outnumbered, that they would probably beat him half to death. He's never scared, even when he has every right to be.

'You touch my sister and I'll kill you,' he said. There was no tone in his voice, no sense of threat as such. It was like he was stating a fact. *The temperature today may reach forty-five degrees. Australia is an island continent. You touch my sister and I'll kill you.* It made it all the more scary. One kid even took a step back.

The girl – Xena? – took a step forward instead and held up her hand.

'Easy soldier,' she said. 'Huge *cojones*, I'll give you that, but your brain's nowhere near as big.' That made all the others laugh. I didn't even know what *cojones* were. 'Brother and sister, huh?' She put her face right up close to Aiden's and examined him as if in search of clues. Then she did the same with me. 'Wow!' She whistled. 'Twins. Something you don't see every day.'

One of the boys, the biggest in fact, stepped in.

'Hey, Xena,' he said. 'Let's stop messing around, okay? Let's just take them to Headquarters. Their parents will trade craploads to get them back and you know it. What the hell are we waiting for?'

Xena put a hand on the boy's shoulder.

'What are we waiting for, Ziggy? What are we waiting for? We're waiting for me to give the order, aren't we? We're waiting for me to make up *my* mind. That's what we're waiting for.'

Like Aiden, she didn't raise her voice but Ziggy turned away regardless. She nodded at the rest of the group and turned back to face me.

'What are you doing here, huh? Why'd you come to the park?'

'Someone said there were mangoes here.' I was still snivelling, so it came out all broken.

That made her laugh. Most of the group gave a chuckle.

'Mangoes?' she said. 'That's the best I've heard in ages. I wish, rich kid. I wish. And what, you thought you'd just wander down here, pluck a couple of juicy mangoes from our park and stroll back to class, huh? Unbelievable.'

'I'm sorry,' I said. I had no idea what I was apologising for. 'Please let us go.' But the other boy had scared me. I hadn't thought of kidnapping. Why hadn't I thought about kidnapping? Our parents were enormously rich, one of the wealthiest couples in New South Wales. Maybe *the* wealthiest. They'd pay a fortune to a kidnapper to get us back and it wouldn't make a dent in their bank account. Suddenly I needed to go to the toilet. My legs started trembling and I really believed I'd wet myself there and then.

Xena smiled.

'Okay,' she said. 'Since you asked so nicely, you can go.'

Ziggy threw up his hands. 'Are you crazy...?' One look from Xena stopped him.

'But hey, rich kids,' she said. 'Stay in school where it's safe, okay? Stay at home with your rich parents in your big house and don't come here again. This here's the real world, you understand? You wouldn't like it here. It's not a place for you.' She turned and walked along the cracked footpath towards the distant trees. The rest of the group followed her a few seconds later. Ziggy was the last. He gave us one last stare. Its hardness was like a punch to the face.

Aiden and I walked past the graffiti on the wall, through the arch and out onto the street. I tried not to look behind and I tried not to run. But when I couldn't keep control anymore, I glanced back. The park was deserted and there was no sign of the street kids. It was as if they'd melted into the landscape.

But I didn't care what my eyes told me. I ran as hard as I could, Aiden keeping pace at my side. We didn't stop until we came to the school fence.

Mr Meredith was waiting for us on the other side.

We were in trouble. But at that moment, it seemed trivial compared to the trouble we'd just been in.

3

Dad drove the car himself, which he only does at times of great stress, when he needs something to do with his hands.

Mr Meredith had rung him when it was discovered we were nowhere in the school grounds. Charlotte hadn't said anything, which was probably good. Going off to find non-existent mangoes would be an embarrassing explanation. Now I could say we just felt like we needed a walk and that we'd only gone a couple of hundred metres before returning. No need to mention being surrounded and nearly kidnapped by a gang of street kids.

Dad sent us to our room as soon as we got home. About the only thing he said was that this was a situation he and Mum would deal with together. He'd get her on his tablet just as soon as she was out of a meeting in Melbourne that couldn't be interrupted. For the next hour Aiden and I would just have to stew.

It turned out to be an hour and a half. We couldn't even use our tablets because Dad had strictly forbidden it, and the library was out of bounds too. Aiden just sat cross-legged on his bed and I guess I should have used the time to talk to him, if only to get our stories straight. But somehow it didn't seem important. I knew Aiden would let me do the talking anyway and that he would echo whatever I said. He'll lie through his teeth to protect me. He's done it before. Many times.

So I spent my time thinking about the girl. I'd never known anyone like her and although I should have been revolted by her dirtiness and the fact she hung out in a gang, I wasn't. She was fascinating. Aiden would probably say that I thought she was fascinating precisely *because* I'd never known anyone like her. Maybe the exotic is always fascinating. Whatever. I couldn't help but imagine the life she led and the history that brought her to that park and into my life, albeit briefly. And why did she just let us go? There didn't seem to be much logic in it.

All my thinking was pointless, of course, because I'd never see her again. But it passed the time.

Dad had made the video call through the media room, so we sat in the front row while Mum's face, two metres high and one metre wide, gazed down on us. She was not happy and the size of the image made her expression even more terrifying. A small part of me registered this as unfair. Our faces and bodies would seem tiny to her. She loomed like a monster.

'I cannot begin to tell you how disappointed I am in you two,' she started. 'What were you thinking? My kids, truants?'

I opened my mouth to speak, but it was obvious my contribution was not going to be welcome, so I shut it again. Mum was like a rollercoaster. She'd started and momentum was building and building. We'd just have to cling on, terrified, until she came to a stop.

'I can't even begin to count the number of times you've been told to obey the rules, that you must not, EVER, go out by yourselves, that the world is a dangerous place, more dangerous than you can begin to imagine and yet, what do you do? Huh? What do you do? You jump over a fence to go off on your own. God knows why.'

I opened my mouth to lie about our motive, but closed it again.

'Anything could have happened to you. You could have been attacked, God forbid, kidnapped or murdered or…' Aiden and I stared at her eyes, blinking only occasionally. 'Are you totally stupid, the pair of you? Or is it that you simply don't care what you've done to us today? Your father was worried sick. He was close to breaking down and sobbing when he rang me and that was *after* you'd been found. I can only imagine what he must have gone through when you were missing, when he got the call from the school. Plus the damage you've done to that teacher. Apparently he was distraught as well, and could quite possibly lose his job over this. And it would all be thanks to you. But you didn't think about that, did you? You didn't stop to think how this would affect anyone else. You only think about yourselves. A pair of selfish brats.'

My eyes filled with tears. Mr Meredith. Mum was right. I hadn't thought that us going off without permission might affect him and it would never have crossed my mind that he could lose his job over it. What had we done?

'So what have you got to say for yourselves, huh?'

And suddenly I found that I *didn't* have anything to say. *I'm sorry?* That wasn't going to cut it, but I couldn't think of anything else.

'I'm so sorry, Mum.'

'Not good enough, Ashleigh Delatour. Not good enough at all.'

'It was my fault.' I'd almost forgotten Aiden was there. I turned towards him, my mouth open. 'It was my fault, Mum,' he continued. 'It was all my idea and Ashleigh didn't want to go but I persuaded her. She tried to talk me out of it. I'm the only one who's to blame.'

There was silence for a good ten seconds. Mum's eyes went from me to Aiden and back again as if weighing our words and our expressions.

'Is this true, Ashleigh?' she asked finally.

'I...' I couldn't think straight. I was being offered a way out. Well, not a way *out*, but a lifeline from complete responsibility. But could I let Aiden take the blame for something that was entirely my idea? Would I have done that if the situation had been reversed? Of course I wouldn't. You'd have to be dumb to plead guilty when you were innocent. And you'd have to be a total bitch to let someone else take the blame, especially your own brother.

'Er, well. Yes. That's true,' I said. 'Mainly.' I kept my eyes fixed to the floor.

No one said anything for the longest time.

'You will go straight to bed after dinner, both of you,' said Mum. 'And there will be no tablet use for a week. You can take books from the library, but that's it. Your father and I will decide whether or not you'll be allowed on the school camp next month. At the moment, I'm inclined to cancel it because it's obvious you can't be trusted. And for all I know the school will cancel your booking for the same reason. We'll talk about it when I get home.'

And she ended the call without even a goodbye.

Dinner was a cheerless affair. No conversation and definitely no chips. When we were done, Dad took us to the library and watched as we selected books to take to our room. The library is just off the swimming pool room. I could see the pool through a window, but I knew there was no point asking if we could swim. Mum had only forbidden tablets, but I knew Dad would add swimming to the list of banned activities, if only because he'd said nothing when Mum was selecting our punishment and he must have felt that he should have had a go too. It's the way I would've felt.

Our library is huge and Mum and Dad are very proud of it. I tried to count all the books once but gave up when I got over twelve thousand because I lost count and couldn't be bothered to start again. Everyone else seems to have books stored electronically and we have that too, of course. But our parents have always said that there is nothing to compete with the feeling of a *real* book in your hands and the sensation of turning pages. High humidity apparently wrecks bindings, so Mum and Dad have the library temperature controlled. There's even an old-fashioned small generator that would keep the place cool when the regular electricity goes out and our batteries fail. Not that that's ever happened in this house. But they're taking no chances. Seems we might have to sweat, but the books must always be cool and comfortable.

I like the old kids' books best, so I took a Shaun Tan from the shelf. His drawings and paintings seem like they're from a different world, one I recognise but can't quite place. When I turn the pages, I turn over my imagination as well as his. Aiden chose a science fiction novel.

We lay in bed reading but for once Tan wasn't able to take me with him. I kept going over the events of the day, the terror, the fascination, the feeling of being deliciously alive in the darkest moments of fear. I worried about Mr Meredith and what I'd say to him in the morning, assuming he hadn't lost his job in the meantime. If he had, I'd bug Mum and Dad to employ him, at a better salary than teaching paid. We could make up a job for him. I couldn't bear to think I was responsible for him being sacked. I knew, I'd been told, that unemployment was so high that the chances of finding employment once you lost it were slim to say the least. Finally, I put the book down on my chest.

'Thank you, Aiden,' I said.

'What for?' He didn't put his book down.

'For protecting me. For taking the blame, saying it was your idea when we both know it was mine.'

'Oh, that.' He turned a page. 'You're welcome.'

'Why did you do it?'

He glanced over at me then. His face was puzzled as if my question was entirely unreasonable, almost unfathomable.

'You said it yourself. To protect you. You'd have done the same for me.'

That doesn't make sense, I thought. *How does that make any kind of sense at all?* Obviously I wouldn't have done the same for him because I could have told the truth, exposed his lie and taken responsibility. But I hadn't.

Sometimes I hate him for making me feel bad about myself. I wonder if he does it deliberately.

After lights out he tried to take my hand, but I wasn't in the mood. I lay in the darkness and listened to thunder rumbling in the distance.

4

'We owe you an apology, Mr Meredith,' I said.

I was so relieved when he popped up in class first lesson, seeming happy and relaxed and most definitely not like someone who was working out his notice. But we had to wait until recess for the opportunity to speak to him privately. Now he looked at us over his glasses, head bowed. I could see a small bald patch on the very top of his scalp. It was sprinkled with dandruff.

'I believe you do,' he replied. No smile. He wasn't going to make this easy for us and I couldn't blame him.

'Sorry, Mr Meredith,' I said.

'Sorry, Mr Meredith,' said Aiden.

'We're so glad you didn't lose your job,' I added.

'Hmmm.' Our teacher took off his glasses and cleaned them with a small cloth he took from his trouser pocket. 'It is easy to say sorry,' he continued, 'and even easier to accept it. Which I do, by the way. Apologies accepted.

But…' He put his glasses back on and regarded us. 'I do wonder if you are really sorry or if an apology is just something you *feel* should be offered.'

I opened my mouth to assure him we were genuine, but he held up a hand.

'What you did was … not safe. My job is not really that important compared to your safety.' He smiled for the first time. 'That's not to say I'm not glad to still have it. And I'm grateful to your parents for ringing up the school board and pleading my case. But you could have died out there. And I would have spent the rest of my life knowing I should have prevented it. You'd be dead, so your suffering would be over. The suffering of your parents, your family and friends would just be beginning. Think about that, Ashleigh and Aiden Delatour, before you do anything like this again.'

We promised we would.

'Then we won't mention it anymore. But I should tell you that you are first up for the oral presentation after recess. You decide which of you is going first.'

Aiden and I glanced at each other in alarm. An oral presentation? This was the first we'd heard of it.

'The first you've heard of it?' said Mr Meredith as if reading our minds. 'That's because the assignment was given out yesterday afternoon. You know, when your father had taken you home. I think you'll find that if this comes as a surprise, it's your fault and your fault only.'

'But we haven't prepared,' I said.

'No,' said our teacher. 'So you'd better use the next fifteen minutes wisely. A two-minute talk on something about you that stands out from the crowd. Now go. The clock is ticking.'

I hate oral presentations at the best of times. Aiden doesn't seem to mind and I figured he wouldn't be fazed by this bombshell. But I could feel my face flush with the first symptoms of panic. We went out to the verandah.

'What are we going to talk about?' I asked.

'I don't know,' he said. 'We'll think of something. Just don't go on about how wealthy we are, okay? Don't talk about the pool or the library or how Mum has her own company and travels the world. People don't like that. They think you're bragging.'

I knew he was right, but it also occurred to me that if I didn't mention those things then how were people expected to know? Anyway, he wasn't helping. I wanted to know what I *should* talk about, not what I shouldn't. I was going to tell him this, but he beat me to it.

'I'll go first to give you a bit more time to prepare. You tell them what it's like to be the eldest of identical twins. That's a subject very few people can talk about.'

For two minutes? I'd be lucky to get to fifteen seconds before running out of stuff to say. I can talk an awful lot at home, according to Mum and Dad, but when I've got loads of people staring at me, I dry up. It's embarrassing. But Aiden was right. I was probably the only expert on this subject for a fifty-kilometre radius. At least.

'The thing that really makes me stand out from the crowd is that I have Klinsmann's disease,' said Aiden.

He stood by the teacher's desk, his hands clasped in front of him. He didn't fidget and his voice was clear and steady. The words didn't pour from his mouth either, like happens with so many kids. His gaze roamed the class, made contact with everyone.

'This is a condition that affects one in approximately twenty million, though most people who have it don't have it as severely as I do.' He held up a hand. 'But don't worry. It's not something you can catch by sitting next to me or by breathing the air around me. You're safe.' He paused and allowed the class to digest this. 'Some of you might think that if I have this disease, then Ashleigh must also have it, since it is generally believed that identical twins have identical DNA.' He looked at Charlotte as he said this. 'But that's not actually true. Sometimes, very very rarely, one identical twin can have a genetic disorder that the other doesn't have. That's because Ashleigh and I have different karyotypes and that means we are *not* genetically identical, though we are in every other way. I'm glad my sister doesn't have this disease, because it's not very pleasant to live with, to tell you the truth.'

He paused again. The class was completely silent and it occurred to me that, although Aiden tends not to say very much most of the time, he certainly knows how to use words when he does. He was keeping the audience guessing about what Klinsmann's disease actually involves. Even Mr Meredith was leaning forward and concentrating and he must have known about Aiden from the medical records Mum and Dad had to provide the school.

'I used to have to go into hospital every few months for treatment for this disease when I was younger,' he said. 'Now that I'm older I don't have to go so often. Once or twice a year. And the surgeons put me to sleep and they operate, cleaning out almost all of my lower intestines.'

I glanced around the class. A few kids grimaced at the mention of intestines, but they were still fascinated.

'You see, that's what Klinsmann's disease does,' Aiden continued. 'It makes it impossible for me to digest food in the way that everyone else can. I could eat an apple, for example, and it would just sit in my stomach. If I ate more, then I would start to feel very uncomfortable. Pain would follow. But most importantly, even with food in my stomach, I'd be starving to death.' He smiled. 'That's not a very good thing, by the way.' A couple of the kids laughed.

'So this is what I eat,' said Aiden. He pulled his dinner flask from his schoolbag and poured a small amount of mush into a bowl that Mr Meredith must have found for him. There was a collective groan of disgust as the green paste settled at the bottom of the bowl. Aiden picked it up and took it to the desk that Charlotte and I shared.

'Pass it around,' he said. 'I know it looks gross, but you could eat it if you want…' There was another groan. 'Smell it. Go on, it won't smell of anything. But it contains everything I need to survive. All the minerals,

43

the calories, the vitamins necessary for survival, but in a form I can digest. Yes?'

A boy towards the back – I hadn't learned his name yet – had his hand in the air. I almost laughed. They were treating Aiden like he was a teacher. I suppose in some ways he was.

'Is that goo *all* you can eat? I mean, *ever*?'

'That's it,' said Aiden. 'And for the rest of my life. So next time you have a pizza or scrambled eggs or even just a plain round of toast, think of me. I can never eat any of that. That goo is, for me, breakfast, lunch and dinner. And afternoon snack.'

Mr Meredith had his hand in the air and the whole class laughed.

'Yes, Mr Meredith?' said Aiden when the laughter had died down.

'So why do you have to go to hospital for operations if that stuff provides all your dietary needs?'

'Because the human intestine wasn't designed for this. After a while there's a build-up of … residue, I guess you'd call it. And if left alone it would clog my gut and stop the digestive process, even for the "goo".'

'Fascinating,' said Mr Meredith. 'An exceptionally good and interesting presentation, Aiden.'

I was disappointed. I wanted Aiden's presentation to go on forever, so I didn't have to get up there. Surely the teacher should've allowed a few more questions? But he didn't. The class gave a round of applause as Aiden walked back to his seat.

My turn.

I stood in front of everyone, but I tried to keep my eyes focused on the top of the window frame at the back of the class. Two minutes had never seemed such a long time. The silence was absolute and that just made me more nervous. I swayed a bit, putting my weight on one leg and then shifting it to the other.

'Ermm,' I said. 'My name is Ashleigh, Ash for short, and what makes me stand out from the crowd is the home I live in. It's more beautiful and more expensive than most people can imagine and I'm going to describe it to you...'

No one applauded when I finished, but at least I got to nearly two minutes. I was so grateful to finally sit down.

Mum's first flight was cancelled because of severe weather in Melbourne, but she was able to get a later one. She had a car waiting for her at the airport in Sydney and Aiden and I were allowed to stay up late for her return, though after the lecture we'd had I wasn't sure if I really wanted to.

As it turned out, most of her anger had evaporated over time. She made it plain that she was still upset with us, but it was more disappointment now.

Dad asked about the conference and she told us that there had been good advances on the use of artificial intelligence in helping some developing countries deal with the effects of climate change. She and Dad had a good chat about it, but I didn't pay a huge amount of attention because it was, to be strictly honest, a bit boring.

Finally, I got the opportunity to bring up the subject I'd been dying to ask about.

'Mum? You said something about a school camp and that we probably wouldn't be allowed to go, but Aiden and I don't know anything about it. What's the camp?'

For a moment I thought Mum was going to tell us to mind our own business, that she and Dad were still going to talk about it and leave us totally in suspense. In fact I could almost see those thought processes flit across her face. But then she obviously decided to put us out of our misery.

'When your father and I enrolled you at school, they said they had a camp planned. In about four weeks, as it turns out. The expectation was that you would both go along.'

Aiden and I looked at each other. Going away without Mum and Dad, with Mr Meredith and the other kids from our class? That sounded beyond awesome.

'And?' I asked.

'It's a five-day camp in the Blue Mountains. Hiking, a bit of horseriding, apparently, and some kayaking. The school has a building up there, very secure against any bad weather that might blow in, as well as trained outback specialists who can keep you safe from wildlife and even gather food if necessary. That's unlikely though, since they take all the comforts with them.'

Dad took over.

'Your class teacher goes with you, as well as a nurse and some pretty tough guys who act as bodyguards in case you meet people who … well, who might not be the kind of people you'd *want* to meet. We were assured it's entirely safe, that everyone has the best time, that you'll fish and barbecue and tell stories over camp fires.' He glanced at Mum. 'It'd better be special, given it costs an arm and a leg.'

'Can we go, please? Please?' I knew Aiden wouldn't beg. He's the kind who'll take his punishment without complaint, but I'm made of different stuff. This sounded totally brilliant and I'd beg on my hands and knees if I had to.

'We haven't decided yet,' said Dad. 'We told you. Your mum and I are going to discuss it and as you well know, she's barely been home five minutes.'

'We're so sorry that Aiden did what he did,' I said. 'Isn't that right, Aiden?' I think he nodded. 'We'll be good as gold, I swear. And this is not an opportunity that comes up very often.' That was an understatement. I'd *never* had an opportunity like this.

'Your father said we'll talk about it,' said Mum. 'Now go to bed, the pair of you. Any more arguing about it, Ashleigh, and I can guarantee that you *won't* be going. You've said good as gold, so put up or shut up. Better still, both.'

I shut up.

That night I let Aiden hold my hand and later I dreamed of camp fires and toasting marshmallows

47

and horseriding and kayak rides through white water. I was smiling as I slept. I know because when I woke up to a morning charged with thunderclouds my face was aching.

5

The tablet-free week dragged on, but it eventually ended.

The first thing I did was look up Xena on the internet. The only reference was to a very old television show about a warrior princess and I guessed the girl in the park had chosen the name for that reason. She was in charge of her group and, judging by the way she put that boy down – what was his name again? Ziggy? – then she was also a warrior and everyone was scared of her. But that's where the resemblance ended. The pictures of the actor from the television show showed someone with long dark hair and a short leather skirt. It was a strange outfit for a warrior who, you'd think, would want to protect her flesh rather than exposing it. Still...

Charlotte was allowed to come for a sleepover on the following Friday night, which was brilliant. Mum and Dad said I couldn't go to her place because I still couldn't be trusted, but I didn't really want to go to hers anyway.

I wanted Charlotte to see *our* house. I showed her round and watched the way her eyes grew bigger as we went from room to room. We finished with a swim, just the two of us. Aiden kept right out of the way. Charlotte wasn't a very good swimmer – it was difficult to get much practice if you didn't own your own pool – so I was able to impress her with my skill.

After dinner, where Dad really showed off by doing a fruit pavlova for dessert, using eggs that Kentucky had laid only that morning and oranges from the tree in the garden, we picked some books from the library and went to bed early. Dad had changed Aiden's sheets (he was going to be sleeping in one of the guest rooms) and Charlotte and I lay and talked. We were never going to do much reading. One of the best things was that I knew Charlotte would be talking about my house to all the other girls in the class on Monday. It wouldn't surprise me if everyone wanted to be my friend... I mean, who wouldn't want to go swimming in a temperature-controlled pool and not have to share it with anyone except me? I'd have to be very careful about who I chose to be a friend. I didn't want girls who were shallow and just going to use me.

We talked about boys. I was shocked to find Charlotte had a crush on Daniel, the boy who'd asked Aiden a question during the oral presentation. He didn't seem very smart to me.

'He isn't,' said Charlotte when I mentioned this, 'but he's so cute.'

Was he? I hadn't realised. Maybe I wasn't paying enough attention to these things.

'Who do *you* think's hot?' she asked.

I pretended to give this some thought, but really I thought most of them were … well, *boys*. The others were … well, *dull* boys.

'I don't want to say,' I replied after a decent enough pause. Charlotte laughed.

'Oh, I see,' she said. 'Is it Jason Bridges?'

Jason Bridges? He had pimples and a huge nose. Should I find him cute?

'I don't want to say,' I repeated, but I gave a small smile that I hoped would pass as mysterious.

The strangest part of our conversation came when we were basically falling asleep, the books slipping part way off the beds.

'Your brother is amazing,' said Charlotte, her voice woolly with tiredness. 'He could have any girl in the class as his girlfriend.'

Really? That woke me up. Something I wouldn't have thought about in a million years. Not surprisingly.

'He's cute,' Charlotte continued. 'But it's his personality that's the most attractive thing about him.'

This conversation was becoming weirder by the moment. I hadn't realised Aiden *had* a personality. I mean, I know he does, but it didn't seem anything out of the ordinary. I kept quiet.

'It's his … *devotion* to you. The way he looks after you, the way he's always checking if you're okay.' She sighed. 'I'd give anything to have someone who felt that way about me. You are so lucky, Ash.'

Lucky? Aiden's devotion normally irritated me, but if Charlotte thought I was lucky, then maybe I needed to give this more consideration. But it was the next thing she said that really threw me.

'Some of the kids in the class think you're really mean about Aiden, you know?' I didn't know. I wasn't mean to him, so how could they think that? And which kids? 'They think you take him for granted, ignore him. Think only about yourself.' She propped herself on an elbow and looked over the gap between beds at me. 'Don't get me wrong. *I* don't think that, Ash. It's just some of the bitchy girls. But I wouldn't be any kind of friend if I didn't tell you what other people think, even if it's people who aren't important. Do you know what I mean?'

I nodded, but I had to bite the inside of my cheek to stop myself from crying. People thought I was mean and selfish? How could they?

We talked a little bit more, about Mr Meredith and the school camp, but her comments had cut me, and though I tried to keep my voice normal, my emotions were bleeding. In the end, I said something and she didn't reply. A few seconds later, I heard her breathing turn rough, like her throat was grating the air.

I could sleep through her snoring. If I could sleep through cyclones I could sleep through her snoring. But I lay awake for the longest time, considering the strange idea that other people might not see me the way I saw myself.

It was troubling.

Mum and Dad agreed that we could go on the school camp. I knew they would, but we had to go through a long period of time where we didn't know for sure. It was part of our punishment. The days before the trip were charged with excitement at school. No one knew what to expect because it was only for our year group and no one had any older siblings, obviously, who could tell them what it was like.

But they'd heard stories.

The night before, Aiden and I packed our bags with Mum and Dad supervising. It was mainly a matter of making sure we had clothing to cope with all kinds of weather conditions, but that was something we were used to. Quite a bit of available space was taken up with Aiden's food. All of us normal kids were being catered for at the camp, but clearly he had to take along everything he was going to eat. The only slight problem was that Aiden was due to go into hospital for one of his routine procedures, but Mum and Dad agreed that he could do that once we got back from the excursion.

We took two books each. There was no point taking tablets. We'd been told that there wouldn't be reception where we were going.

Mum and Dad drove us to school on the Monday morning of the trip and it was chaotic outside the building. Everyone else's parents were there and bags were strewn all over the place and people were hugging each other and there were people with clipboards and people in uniform and … Well, it was enough to take your breath away.

'Have the best time, kiddlypunks,' said Mum. She had a meeting and couldn't hang around to say goodbye when we actually left. That was okay. At least she said it quietly and left with a minimum of fuss. Dad went at the same time.

Then the coach turned up. It was amazing. It looked like a normal coach, but I knew from Mum and Dad talking about it that it was state of the art. There were steel shutters that could cover the windows in case of an unexpected event and apparently it was more like a tank than a regular coach. You could fall off a cliff and be safe, though I hoped that wouldn't be tested.

There was so much paperwork to be filled out, but finally everything was in order and we boarded the coach. Charlotte was a little ahead of me in the queue and as I went past she patted the seat next to her. I stopped, thus blocking the gangway and making everyone behind me stop as well.

'Thanks Charlotte,' I said, 'but I think I'll sit with Aiden. I mean, I won't have much chance to be with him when we're all in our dormitories.' I spoke quite loudly and the bus had an echo to it. Aiden seemed a little surprised. He turned and gave me a bit of a strange look. But it was obvious he was pleased.

We sat towards the back of the coach and he tried to hold my hand but I wasn't having any of that. It's not like we were six years old.

Mr Meredith walked up and down the coach, yet another clipboard in his hand, checking off names one last time. Or so I supposed. He gave us a smile as he passed.

'Excited?' he said.

I was going to try to be cool, but then thought it wouldn't make any difference.

'Yes,' I said. 'Very.'

'Good. You should be.'

And then he was gone, ticking boxes on his clipboard.

Finally, we set off. We even had a proper driver, a man with a peaked cap who smiled at all of us before taking his seat at the front and starting the engine.

We drove away from the school and down Albert Street, towards the park. As we swept by it, I thought I saw a small girl sitting under a Moreton Bay fig in the furthest corner. But it was a long way away and it might have been my imagination.

The journey took just over an hour and a half and we spent all of the time glued to the windows watching the landscape as it scrolled past. Aiden swapped seats with me so I could get the best view and I made sure I thanked him. It was probably the longest journey we'd taken since we moved to Sydney three years ago and I'd forgotten most of that.

There was hardly any traffic on the road and a good few of the suburbs we passed seemed as if they'd seen better days. Some buildings were abandoned and crumbling, but whether that was due to neglect or the result of an occasional tornado was impossible to say.

It didn't take too long before we left all buildings behind and started to see more of the countryside. Like parts of Sydney, some places appeared to be green and flourishing, while others were a bit sad. But it was all so strange that none of it mattered. The driver put music on and it wasn't long before everyone was singing and clapping. It was obvious that my classmates were as excited as me.

Eventually, we took a side road and bumped over an uneven, potholed track for a couple of kilometres. All the kids groaned as we hit a bump and we made a game of who could groan the loudest, so that by the time we stopped the coach was ringing with the sound of kids moaning and laughing. It was so much fun. But then, as we realised we'd reached our destination, we stopped, and the silence was deafening. We all peered out the window.

The coach had stopped in a fenced clearing in front of a large wooden building with a wraparound verandah. There was one door, close to where we'd stopped, flanked by a few barred windows. I was on the side of the coach furthest from the building and when I looked to my right

I saw a man in uniform close the chain link gates and lock them. I hadn't even realised we'd come through any gates.

We stayed on board for another five minutes while Mr Meredith and a couple of the security guards checked the building and the grounds. We'd been told to call the guards 'camp assistants', but that didn't really fool anyone, mainly because they were all large and unsmiling and had guns in holsters around their waists. I imagined they were checking the place in case anyone had broken in, though we were so far from civilisation that it seemed unlikely anyone would have made the trek. Then again, there was apparently five days' worth of food for twenty-five kids stashed in there, not to mention medicines and other luxury items, so it would've been an attractive target for thieves. Anyway, it seemed the coast was clear because Mr Meredith stepped up into the coach and addressed us.

'As you must have worked out, we are here,' he said, smiling. 'This is home for the next five days. Your luggage is being taken out of the hold as I speak and I ask that you claim your bags first. Then the boys will follow me and the girls will follow Ms Anderson and we will show you where you are sleeping. Once you have made yourselves comfortable and unpacked whatever needs unpacking, we will have lunch and Ms Anderson and I will tell you about the activities for the rest of the day. Any questions?'

There weren't, so we filed down the bus's steps and made our way to the mound of luggage that the driver had emptied from the belly of the coach. I had only one smallish bag and Aiden's wasn't much bigger and we managed to get through the scrum of kids to pick them up. I was the first to line up behind Ms Anderson, a small woman with unnaturally dark hair and a large hairy mole on the left side of her face. She smiled at me, but it didn't shed much warmth. I didn't know who Ms Anderson was, but guessed she might have been a teacher from another year level. Perhaps she was the principal. I suppose I could've asked her, but her expression didn't invite questions. Already I was missing Mr Meredith and we hadn't really started the camp yet.

Sixteen girls eventually got their stuff and lined up behind me. Charlotte was towards the back because she'd brought three suitcases. When Dad saw her at the school he'd made some comment about bringing the kitchen sink, but he doesn't really know what girls need when they go away from home. I would've taken loads more if my parents hadn't stopped me.

The dormitory was large with a high ceiling fretted by wooden beams. Old-fashioned electric lights dangled occasionally from the rafters, though they were turned off. Two barred windows spilled light onto polished floors and twenty or thirty bunk beds were lined up along the walls. Ms Anderson said we could choose, so Charlotte and I picked a bunk close to the toilets and shower. It was only later that I wondered if this was wise. After we'd put our stuff in lockers beside the bunks, we took our toiletries into the bathroom. There were five toilets and five shower cubicles. Ms Anderson said we would have to negotiate the use of both and that this was one of the aims of the camp, to instil a sense of cooperation among students who might find that a challenging and maybe unique proposition. I didn't quite understand what she meant by that.

Lunch was fairly basic, just some bread rolls with a selection of cheeses and processed meat-substitutes. We ate outside on the verandah, and although some kids tried to sit in the open air, Mr Meredith shooed them into the shade. Aiden stayed inside to eat his green, snot-looking goo. He understands that it often grosses people out if they see him eating it. He's considerate that way. When we'd finished, Mr Meredith called us to order.

'Welcome to camp,' he said. 'You are going to have a wonderful time over the next five days, I guarantee it. Back in the day, many schools would have camps but now there's only one school in the whole of Sydney that provides this service to its Year Eights. If you can't work out which school this is, then I can't help you and maybe you should give up any hope of getting a decent education.'

We laughed in a sort of dutiful way and Ms Anderson took over.

'A few housekeeping rules,' she said. 'You know the toilets are in your dormitories and I shouldn't have to tell you that boys are restricted to their area and girls are restricted to theirs. Anyone found breaking this rule will be sent home immediately. Each day we will be engaged in a separate activity. This afternoon we will be going for a short hike in the bush – about a kilometre and a half, that's all – to a small lake where you can swim.' There was a murmur of excitement and she held up her hand. 'Bring your bathers when we assemble in about an hour. Mr Meredith and I will provide sunblock, hats and T-shirts for anyone who forgot to pack those items. You cannot swim until we give you permission that it is safe to do so. Anyone breaking this rule will be sent home immediately.'

There was quite a bit more. How we didn't have any signals for tablets out here and that as a result we wouldn't be travelling far from the camp, in case the weather turned nasty and we had to make it back to safety in a hurry. Most importantly, we had to follow all instructions by all adults during our stay at camp.

'If anyone fails to do this...' said Mr Meredith. 'Well, you can guess the rest.' He smiled and we smiled, though not with the same strength. I think we were all keen to get out of the building and into the fresh air. But we had to wait an hour. For our food to digest, said Mr Meredith. You can't go swimming on a full stomach, said Ms Anderson. You can get cramps. I didn't believe any of that. I'd swum plenty of times after lunch and it had never affected me. But there was nothing I could do. Even after the hour passed it took time to get going because we all had to be inspected by the teachers to make sure we had on sufficient sunblock and that our hats were big enough to keep the sun from our face, neck and shoulders. One girl tried wearing a short-sleeved T-shirt but she was made to change. Finally, we all trooped out into the early afternoon sunshine.

One of the camp assistants unlocked another gate at the back of the property and we filed through, Ms Anderson taking the lead, the class following and Mr Meredith and another assistant at the rear. Charlotte and I stayed towards the back. Aiden walked by himself a few metres ahead of us, glancing over his shoulder from time to time. I gave him a hard stare when he'd done this about ten times and after that he didn't check on me quite so much.

The walk was wonderful. None of us really got out into nature very much and although our garden at home was very big and secure, it wasn't quite the same as being in what seemed to us a wilderness. Mr Meredith would occasionally point out certain types of trees as we passed them. He even had a go at identifying birds from their calls alone, and we spied a couple of raptors circling over us at one point, which was very exciting. I kept an eye out for snakes, but Mr M assured me that the chances of stumbling across one were remote. That didn't stop me looking, though.

The lake wasn't really a lake, more of a waterhole, but it was beautiful, with shades of green and blue reflecting from the water. At the far end there was a rock face that rose straight up and a waterfall splashed from about ten metres over our heads, providing a natural shower, thousands of droplets dimpling the surface and rainbows pulsing into and out of existence. The whole class stood still for a couple of seconds and then we were all frantically getting our pants or dresses off. The teachers tried to tell us something about the depth of the water and to take care, but no one was listening. About ten of us hit the water at the same time and the cold made us gasp. It was a delicious change from the humidity and there was much whooping and shouting as the rest of the class joined us. Probably because I live in a house with a pool, I was the first to make it to the far end and I floated on my back, letting the waterfall pound my face. Aiden joined me a few moments later and we lay, head to head, blinking through the downpour into an impossibly blue sky. I laughed, but that turned to spluttering as I discovered it's not a good idea to open your mouth under a waterfall. Then a whole bunch of kids turned up and that put an end to the floating.

We spent three hours in that waterhole and I reckon we could've spent at least three more, but Mr Meredith and Ms Anderson made us get out and dry ourselves off before the walk back.

'I know, I know,' said Mr Meredith as we all protested and pleaded for some extra time. 'But we have to get back, get showered and get ready for dinner.' He put a finger to his chin. 'Or do you not want a barbecue tonight? No sizzling soy sausages and fried onions and veggieburgers and toasted marshmallows for dessert? Well, if you're sure that's what you want. Or rather, what you *don't* want...'

And that, of course, produced howls of protest and laughter. So we dried ourselves as best we could – our shirts would probably dry on our backs in about five minutes while we walked – and set off on the return journey. Once again, Charlotte and I stayed at the rear of the group, just behind Ms Anderson this time and a hundred metres in front of two camp assistants who ambled along looking bored. After a few minutes, I pulled on Charlotte's sleeve and put a finger to my lips when she turned to look at me.

'I'm bursting for a wee, Charlotte,' I whispered.

'Well, let's hurry,' she said. 'It can only be ten minutes to camp.'

'I can't wait ten minutes.'

Charlotte sighed. 'Well, duck behind those bushes,' she said. 'I'll keep watch for you.'

'Come with me. Please? What if there are snakes? Please, Charlotte?'

'There won't be snakes. You heard Mr Meredith.'

'But what if he's wrong? Please? I'll be quick.'

She sighed again. 'All right, you big baby. But you'd *better* be quick.'

And I was. Charlotte stood with her back to me while I pulled my knickers down and squatted behind one of the huge bushes that lined the track. What a relief. I was just about to get up when I heard voices in a murmured conversation. In the emergency that was my bladder I'd forgotten about the two assistants following behind and it was clear they hadn't seen us leave the track, maybe because we'd just turned a bend. When I poked my head out carefully, they were standing on the track, smoking. And talking.

'Tellya, there's gotta be a better way of earning a living than this,' said one.

'Mate, it ain't exactly hard yakka,' replied the other.

'Nah. That's not what I meant. It's easy work, sure. But it hurts me, mate, it hurts me to be babysitting these spoiled rich brats.'

'They're just kids and it's not their fault. Give 'em a break, man.'

The first man inhaled and blew out a cloud of bluish-grey smoke.

'I know it's not their fault and I'm not gonna say anything, but I'm just sayin' to you; there are starvin' kids all over Australia, let alone the world, and these ones here ... well, you heard that teacher. Sausages, burgers, toasted fricken marshmallows for God's sake. It's not right. That's all I'm sayin'. It's not right.'

The other man clapped him on the shoulder.

'No argument from me,' he said. 'But it's the way it is and you and me, we have no say in how the world goes, mate. No power. So keep your head down and do your job. Who knows? Maybe the odd soy sausage could slip accidentally into your pocket. Just get food on *your* family's table. You'll find that's worth a whole world of hurt feelings.'

The other man snorted. 'I hate you, mate.'

'No, you don't. Come on. Stub out that smoke and let's catch up.' He laughed. 'Maybe one of those brats will get a blister and if we're not on duty it'll be our fault. They might shoot us.'

And in thirty seconds they were gone. I turned to Charlotte and saw the anger in her face that was probably a reflection of mine. I could feel a hot flush on my cheeks and my teeth were grinding so hard they hurt.

'They can't call us that,' I said.

'"Spoiled brats",' said Charlotte. 'How dare they? How dare they? We have to tell Mr Meredith, Ash. I don't want those men around me. Around us. I want them gone. My dad will be so angry when I tell him. More than anyone, he knows that security guards shouldn't speak like that. It's totally unprofessional.'

'I agree,' I said. 'And I think Mr Meredith is going to be *so* mad with them.'

'I see,' said Mr Meredith. We'd asked to have a private word with him, while the rest of the students showered and changed for the barbecue, and he'd taken us outside to an eating area with tables and benches already set up for dinner. There was no one else around. 'And you want to make a formal complaint?'

'Yes,' said Charlotte. 'Definitely.'

'Yes,' I said.

'Hmmm. That is, of course, your right, ladies.' He sat at one of the benches and toyed with a fork, head bent. Charlotte and I sat opposite. I'd calmed down a little, but I knew we were doing the right thing. Those men were paid by the school, but the school was paid by my parents. They worked for us and should therefore have respect. It wasn't good enough to be horrible about us behind our backs while they took our money. Plus, they were planning to steal some of our food. It wasn't fair, especially when apparently there were plenty of other men, *honest* men probably, looking for work. Charlotte made these points to Mr Meredith quite forcefully. I found myself nodding as she talked.

'Okay,' said Mr Meredith when Charlotte was done. 'I hear you loud and clear. But can I ask one favour?' He didn't wait for a reply, but carried straight on. 'Keep this to yourselves for the time being, okay? I don't want other students hearing about this, maybe saying something to the assistants. That would not be good for morale in camp and it is my duty to make sure that all the students enjoy themselves without worrying about anything, if that is possible.' He put the fork down and looked us straight in the eyes. 'I would take your silence on this matter for the rest of our stay as a personal favour. Do you understand?'

We nodded and he smiled.

'Then your complaint is registered, girls, and will be dealt with. I hope, however, you can put this unpleasant-ness to one side and enjoy the rest of the camp.'

We stood and I remembered feeling pleased that we had made a stand. But it seemed Mr Meredith wasn't done with me just yet, because he asked if he could have a word with me in private. Charlotte looked slightly put out but there wasn't much either of us could do, so she walked back to the camp hut and I sat down again. Mr Meredith went back to toying with the fork and for a minute or two there was silence. Then he glanced up at me and smiled.

'Do you want to see something marvellous, Ashleigh?' he said.

I nodded. He placed the fork back down carefully in its place, stood and walked over to the far reaches of the area in front of the building, to the right of the entrance gates, still securely padlocked. I followed. Mr M stopped and pointed into the bush.

'What do you think of that?' he asked.

I squinted, but couldn't see anything out of the ordinary.

'I can't see...' But then I could. It must have been the slight movement of my head and the way the setting sun was positioned, but I saw it and it almost took my breath away. A huge web, at least a metre in diameter, interlocking filaments glowing golden in the dying light. And there, right at the centre, was a massive spider, its legs long and splayed, mottled red, grey and black, its swollen abdomen gunmetal grey. The web shimmered slightly in the breeze and gold danced in the evening light. I wasn't scared. Maybe I should've been. This was the biggest spider I had ever seen and its web looked big enough and strong enough that if I put my hand into it, I might never pry it loose. But it was so beautiful.

'A golden orb-weaving spider,' said Mr Meredith. 'Isn't it magnificent?'

I nodded.

'They used to be really common in Australia,' he continued, 'but changes in the climate over the last fifty years have drastically reduced their numbers. Like so many insects and animals. I thought you'd like it, Ashleigh.'

'It's stunning.'

Mr Meredith took a step towards the web and beckoned me closer. I followed, but cautiously. The spider *was* colossal and trembled slightly in the centre of its home, like it might be preparing to jump. But I trusted my teacher to keep me safe.

'See there, Ashleigh?' he said. 'At the top of the web?'

It was another spider, a tiny one this time. Maybe it had been caught itself and was moments away from becoming a meal.

'That's the male,' said Mr M. 'Weird, isn't it, the difference in size between the female in the centre and the male hanging around the edge? Oh, and see those little bundles of silk lined up just beneath the male? That's the larder. Insects caught in the web that the female has wrapped up for dinner later.'

I found my mouth was hanging open, so I shut it.

'Some creatures in nature have the most beautiful, intricate homes,' he continued. 'Glorious creations that they built themselves with hard work, skill and against all odds.' He put a hand on my shoulder. 'Makes you feel quite humble, doesn't it?'

I nodded.

'Please don't tell the other children about this, Ashleigh,' Mr Meredith added. 'Though your brother would be an obvious exception, if you insist he keeps it secret as well. You see, some people might destroy it, rip the web apart, not because the spider is doing them any harm, but because they have the power. Some people, sadly, like to wield power. And I'm not sure if we could live with ourselves if we ripped up the life of another living creature for no good reason at all. You're not that kind of person, are you, Ashleigh?'

'No, Mr Meredith,' I said.

He smiled. 'I thought not. I'm a good judge of character.'

We'd returned to the dining area by this time and other kids were coming out to take their places. The assistant who'd smoked on the walk back was getting the barbecue ready, checking the gas bottle and scraping stuff off the grills. He smiled as one of the kids asked him something.

Mr Meredith squatted down in front of me.

'That's Mr Dyson,' he said. 'Do you remember the Sydney bushfires about ten years ago?' He shook his head and laughed. 'Of course you don't remember. You'd only be two years old. I'm an idiot. Well, there were hundreds and hundreds of deaths. It was a huge tragedy, one of the worst in a couple of decades. Mr Dyson lost his wife to those fires. Now he's bringing up their son by himself. He's being looked after by a neighbour while Mr Dyson is here with us. I know he misses his son, but what can you do? A man has to earn a living.'

He straightened and clapped his hands.

'Well, off with you, child. Shower and then out here for dinner.' I turned to go. 'Oh, and Ashleigh?' he added. I turned back. 'It's great to see you and Charlotte becoming friends. She needs someone to talk to about important things.'

I smiled, nodded and went into the dormitory. I was excited and not just by the prospect of the barbecue. Mr Meredith and I shared a secret, one I could reveal only to Aiden. He was going to be so excited when I showed him. He loves everything to do with animals and nature.

6

I had the weirdest dream.

Mum and Dad were trying to tell me something, but they were talking to me behind a huge glass wall. I could see their lips moving, but no sound came through. And then I realised why. I was inside a massive aquarium. I glanced down and saw that my feet were dangling and my arms were making small circular motions to help me tread water. My face was pressed up against the glass. It felt good to be weightless. And then I noticed air bubbles fizzing against my cheeks and climbing upwards. They were coming from the corner of my mouth and when I tilted my head back and looked up, I couldn't see the water's surface. The trail of bubbles rose and disappeared into a grey murk above me.

Mum and Dad were signalling, their faces twisted in worry, but I wasn't sure why. I felt good. I felt happy. And then I saw Aiden on the other side of the glass with my parents and all of my good mood escaped, streamed away like bubbles of air. He should be with me. How could he look after me if he was on the other side? I opened my mouth to tell him and the water slammed down my throat. I inhaled it and it felt like stones churning and tumbling in my lungs…

I sat bolt upright in bed and it took me at least a minute to realise where I was. Sweat dripped down my face and my breathing was heavy. I guess it was lucky I hadn't cried out. No one else in the girls' dormitory seemed to be awake. After a few moments I could hear gentle snoring beneath me and somewhere off to my right. I lay down and tried to get back to sleep, but the dream was so vivid I had difficulty scrubbing it from my mind. Eventually, though, I drifted off and if I dreamed again, I wasn't aware of it.

I managed to get Aiden to see the web right after breakfast and he was thrilled. He kept staring at it, saying, 'Oh, my God, Ash. Oh, my God.'

'You can't tell anyone, okay?' I said.

He just nodded and I knew he wouldn't. If there's one thing about Aiden it's that if he makes a promise nothing will get him to break it. So I watched him watching the web and it was like watching myself when I first saw it. I imagined Aiden's reactions would be a perfect mirror of my own. Sometimes I think having a twin is like having a video of yourself or a hologram walking at your side. Weird in a way, but also great.

Breakfast was just some toast and a selection of jams and marmalades, but that was okay. I think most of us were still stuffed after the barbecue, which had been amazing. A couple of my classmates over-indulged on the marshmallows – Charlotte and I had a laugh when we heard them throwing up in the toilets later. After breakfast, Ms Anderson and Mr M called us to order outside and told us what we'd be doing that day. Day two of our camp. I was kinda hoping that horseriding would be today because I'd never ridden a horse and it was a bit of an ambition of mine. In the programs I'd watched it seemed really exciting, if a little scary. I hoped they'd have small horses to fit the size of us. Falling off a big horse, I guessed, would *hurt*.

Turns out horseriding was for the following day. Today we'd be kayaking, something else I'd never done, so that was good. Plus it was another water activity and I'm comfortable in water. The trek today was slightly longer than to the waterhole and we were warned that we'd have to hike across some rough land. Apparently there was a rocky scree leading down to the water's edge that was quite steep, so we all had to wear hiking boots. The assistants, we were told, had already carried the four kayaks down to the river while we had breakfast, so we just had to wait for their return before setting off. They would also carry our food – because there were only four kayaks and twenty-five of us, we'd be taking it in turns and that meant we'd spend nearly the whole day out there.

Our teachers handed out bright orange life jackets that we'd carry.

'Do not put them on until we get there,' said Mr Meredith. 'It looks like it's going to be another hot one today and we don't want anyone passing out with heatstroke. And, as always, drink lots of water, and wear sunscreen and hats all the time.'

We all joined in on a chorus of those last three words. The whole sentence was something that you could put on our gravestones.

Charlotte wanted me to walk with her when we set off, but I told her I had to talk to my brother about something important. I promised I'd walk back with her though, but she still didn't look very pleased. So Aiden and I took up our position at the back, which was getting to be a bit of a habit for me. But it was a good place to talk without being overheard, and I needed to run a few ideas by him.

'Kayaking, hey, Ash?' he said after a hundred metres of silence. 'I'm looking forward to that.'

'Me too, Aiden. Should be fun.' I wiped sweat from my forehead with my sleeve. Mr Meredith was right. It was another hot one today already. 'Aiden?' I said. 'Do you think we're spoiled brats?'

'What makes you ask that?'

So I told him about what Charlotte and I had overheard on the trail yesterday. I kept my eyes on his face as I talked, just to see if he was still a mirror of my emotions.

This time, it seemed, he wasn't, because his expression didn't really change.

'Don't you think that's unfair?' I asked, when the story was told. I didn't tell him about the talk we'd had with Mr Meredith afterwards.

'Maybe the brat bit,' Aiden replied. 'Not sure that's a conclusion he could come to with the information he's got.'

'Mum called us that after we went to the park. She said we were selfish brats.'

'Yeah, but she *did* have the evidence. I don't think this guy knows us as well as Mum.'

'But he also called us spoiled. Spoiled?'

'Oh, yeah. That's a fair comment.'

'Seriously?'

'Of course, seriously. There's no way you could argue we aren't spoiled, Ashleigh. I mean, come on. You must know we're crazily privileged.'

'But that's something Mum and Dad have worked very hard for. Well, Mum, I mean. She's obviously the one bringing in the money.' Dad didn't work. As he liked to remind us almost constantly, he is the househusband charged with keeping everything and everyone neat, tidy, fed and watered. Mum had offered to provide household help with the latest AI devices her company produced, but he'd turned them all down. *What would I do then?* he'd asked. *Lie around and get fat?* He saw Mum open her mouth, so he added, *fatter?* She just laughed and let the subject drop. Sometimes, though, I wished Dad would let her bring some of her inventions home. By all accounts, they are incredibly cool. I was so busy thinking all this that I missed Aiden's reply.

'What?' I said.

'I said it doesn't matter how hard Mum works, we have money and things that ninety-nine point nine per cent of people can only dream of. And even if I accept that Mum deserves it, *we* don't. We were just lucky enough to be born into the right family. Yup. Spoiled is a pretty mild term for it.'

'So you don't think I should report that man for what he said?'

Aiden looked at me as if trying to work out if I was serious.

'Hey,' he said finally. 'Pretty thin skin there, Ash. Of course you shouldn't report him. He'd probably lose his job. I don't think we're *that* spoiled that we would like to see someone else suffer just because we can.'

I lapsed into silence. Aiden's words mingled with Mr Meredith's from last night and I was confused. This was something I'd really have to think through.

'Thanks, Aiden,' I said. 'You've given me a lot to think about.'

'Excellent,' he said. 'I'm all in favour of thinking.'

'I'm going to join Charlotte now.'

He waved a hand at me.

'Missing you already,' he said.

He can be such a smart alec sometimes.

Kayaks are *dangerously* unstable. I discovered this when I was doing my practice runs at the part of the river that was little more than a sluggish pool. I don't think any of us had done kayaking before, but I suspect it wouldn't have mattered if we had. Mr Meredith and Ms Anderson insisted we go through all the safety procedures, like how to right the kayak if we capsized. I was more concerned about getting *out* of it if I capsized. To be honest, losing a kayak wasn't something I was too bothered about. Mum could buy them another twenty. They told us things like, if we fell out, to stay upstream of the kayak to avoid getting pinned between the boat and a rock and to hold on to it for flotation until one of the assistants came to help.

'Never try to stand up in a kayak,' said Mr Meredith to the whole group. Was he mad? Who in their right mind would want to stand up in something so small and flimsy? I was scared just trying to fit into it and when I did, it wobbled from side to side in a frightening way.

It took nearly two hours for all of us to practise getting in and out of the four kayaks and there was plenty of laughing and screaming when people fell into the shallow water. That didn't matter. It cooled us down. I tried the paddle and even managed to keep the kayak in a fairly straight line for the ten or so metres we were allowed to travel before giving someone else a turn. Finally, Mr Meredith decided we knew the safety basics and had enough experience to take them out for a proper go.

The river was very placid where we were, though the current picked up maybe four hundred metres downstream. Far off in the distance I could just make out some white water, presumably where the gradient increased and there were rocks and boulders forming rapids. We weren't going anywhere near that, which was a relief. The idea was that three of us kids would go out at a time, with one kayak being taken by a camp assistant who was there to monitor us and make sure if someone did fall in, he could bring them back. But we were told that it would be difficult to fall out in the stretch of river we were using. Paddle a couple of hundred metres, turn around and paddle back, do that for about half an hour and then give someone else a go. A few of the kids were disappointed and thought it was too easy, but Mr Meredith said that if we all did well, there was a chance that we could go through a small rapid at the end of the day. I thought I might give that a miss, though I would've put money on Aiden being keen.

We were the second-to-last group to head out; me, Charlotte and Aiden and a female camp assistant whose name I didn't know. To be honest, I'd preferred the waterhole. I mean, it was okay paddling about but Mr Meredith was right – there was no wind to speak of, the surface of the water was extremely calm and there was no chance of falling in, which would not have been bad, actually, as it was hot and the combination of using the paddle and wearing a life jacket meant I was dripping with sweat. I stopped for a while and drifted, put my head up to the clear blue sky and let my arm muscles relax. Charlotte drifted up next to me.

'Not much to it, is there?' she said. She pointed towards the distant rapids. '*That* would be exciting, but this is strictly for tiny kids. We should have stuck to video games. Way more fun and we wouldn't be half boiled to death.'

'Race you back?' I replied.

'Okay. Might as well get a bit competitive. But I'm gonna kick your skinny butt, Ash. You should know that.'

'In your dreams, girl.'

Actually, it wasn't in her dreams. The three of us lined up on an imaginary starting line and Aiden did the countdown to go. I wasn't worried about him beating us. I imagined he could if he wanted, but he'd always let me win and I thought it was probable he'd do the same for Charlotte.

'Two, one, GO!' shouted Aiden and I bent my paddle into the water, pulled and then did the same on the other side. But occasionally my coordination leaves something to be desired. I don't even have to think about the rhythm when I'm swimming, but kayaking, I discovered, was different. I smacked my paddle against the side of the boat as I was bringing it over and the next thing I knew it was wrenched from my grip and floating in the water. Not a big problem because it was right by the kayak, but by the time I'd fished it out, Aiden and Charlotte were ten metres ahead and they had momentum. I was wallowing and it was obvious I was going to lose this race, big time. But I gripped the paddle and tensed my muscles for the pursuit.

What came next seemed to happen in slow motion. Or rather, the first part was like that, before the whole world turned upside down and time lost meaning. I remember I was arcing the paddle to my right and had just felt it bite the water, when darkness swept over me. It wasn't total darkness, but the day had been so bright that it almost seemed that way. Now a band of gloom raced past, overtaking Charlotte and Aiden in less than a second. It must be a scudding cloud, I remember thinking, though the sky, up to this point, had been clear. I tilted my head, eyes adjusting to the sudden change in light. Somewhere in the back of my mind I was aware of a light breeze where before the day had been still. I expected to see a raincloud. What I didn't expect was a swirling dance of leaves and debris so dense it blotted out the sun.

I turned to my left, the kayak starting to rock as the wind picked up speed. Grit and dirt splattered against my face. I narrowed my eyes, but even so I could still see it. A twisting mass of orange and grey spiralling across the bank, dipping into the water and heading towards me. It was hypnotic. Somewhere, someone shouted a warning. Even then, I wasn't aware of being in danger. Not really. It was all so unexpected, so...*alien*. A corkscrewing wind, picking up litter from the bank. Weird. Not life-threatening.

I probably thought this for less than a second, before a shearing gale twisted the kayak round in a tight circle. The paddle was ripped from my grasp. And then I was in the middle of a power that wiped out everything else.

I was blind and the screaming wind deafened me. It took a few seconds to realise the boat was gone, that I was in the water, tumbling over and over. I opened my eyes, though I couldn't remember having closed them, but all I could see were bubbles as the water churned the darkened world to white. It wasn't even possible to see what was up and what was down, so I didn't know which way to swim. Not that I *could* swim; the river was alive and taking me wherever it wished. I hadn't even had time to take a breath of air and although I could only have been underwater for a very short time, my lungs already ached and I had to resist the urge to inhale. I kicked and moved my arms. A small part of me was still functioning, it seemed, and I guessed that if I could move anywhere away from that spiralling column, then I might find calmer water and get my head above the surface. But with no sense of direction, it was hard and I was panicking and no matter what I did I couldn't seem to get away from whatever force was playing with me, throwing me around like a child's toy, drawing me deeper and deeper towards... well, towards death.

Suddenly I understood. I was going to die here and it didn't matter what I did. This watery embrace was the last I would ever feel. And with that realisation came a great sense of peace. It would be easy. All I needed to do was take a great deep breath of water and it would be all over. It wasn't so bad. It really wasn't so bad. I think I might even have smiled.

The hand gripped me by the hair and pulled and the pain brought me back to myself. My lungs were on the brink of giving up but I held my breath just a little longer. And then my head was above water and I inhaled, the air sweet and clean and wonderful. I went under again and this time choked, before coming up once more, spluttering and spitting.

Aiden's face was close to mine. He'd let go of my hair and he had an arm around my chest and up under my armpit. We went below the surface once more and I was so, so tired. I wanted to help him help me, but I didn't know how. So I stayed limp and gave him control. He'd know what to do. Aiden always knows what to do.

When we hit the rock I thought I had broken every one of my ribs. The pain was intense, but like before it reminded me I was alive and that the alternative to pain wasn't so good after all. I grabbed the rock and it was slippery and my fingers could barely find a hold. Aiden was wedged next to me and I could see on his face how he was thinking everything through. He watched as my grip slipped even more and both of us knew that if I was swept away he'd never be able to catch me. Not again. I couldn't be saved twice. So I closed my eyes, held on as tightly as possible and prayed to a God I didn't even know I believed in.

Something tightened round my neck and I opened my eyes. Aiden had somehow managed to get his life jacket off and he had looped it around the top of the rock, clicking the belt attachment closed around my neck, effectively tying me in place. My hold finally gave way and the swirling current churned me around, but

I stayed fixed to the rock. I twisted some more, since I now couldn't see my brother. How could he survive in this without a life jacket? I wasn't sure I was going to and I had two. As I struggled to see, I felt an arm and I grabbed hold as it fell away from me. Then I found his fingers. Finally, I caught a glimpse of his face. It was scared and cut and his eyes found mine and maybe he tried to say something, I don't know, because the water was boiling and the sound was deafening and my grip on him was loosening and I couldn't do anything, I couldn't even cry out as a surge of water broke us apart and he disappeared, just disappeared; where once he had been, there was nothing now but churning white and hopelessness. I closed my eyes and screamed, but the world swallowed it.

It was Mr Dyson who swam and got me off that rock, dragged me to the river edge and cleared my airways, but I don't remember much of that. It was also Mr Dyson who carried me back to camp, while nearly everyone else searched for Aiden, but I don't remember that either. It was Mr Dyson who drove the coach the twenty kilometres necessary to call emergency services, but I guess there's no way I would ever have known that in the normal course of events.

When I opened my eyes, I saw Mr Meredith. I tried to speak but my throat was raw and bruised and I couldn't say anything. But he knew what I wanted to ask.

'We're still looking for Aiden, Ash,' he said. He must have seen the pain in my eyes, because he added, 'He's a tough one, your brother. Try not to worry.' But then he turned his face away as if embarrassed by his own words. I felt a sob rising in my throat but I couldn't even cry. So I closed my eyes again and saw my brother's face just before it was snatched away.

The helicopter took me straight to hospital, where Mum and Dad were waiting for me. They held my hands as I was wheeled in and Mum was fighting really hard not to cry. I'd got a little of my voice back by this time, so I asked about Aiden. Mum shook her head.

'Still searching, Ash,' she whispered. 'But don't give up hope.' She tried to smile, but it came out all wrong. 'We mustn't give up.'

I was given painkillers, which helped, and taken to x-ray where it was discovered I had cracked a couple of ribs but hadn't broken anything else. The doctor said they were going to keep me in for a few days to make sure I hadn't done any serious damage, to 'monitor my condition', but she told me she thought I was going to be fine. I didn't feel fine. I felt tired and defeated. I didn't want to sleep until I had some news about Aiden, but the drugs they'd given me took away what little energy remained. I closed my eyes. My sleep was dreamless.

When I woke, it was with a jolt that brought the pain back all new and refreshed. I groaned. Dad was at my bedside and was holding my hand. He was also smiling.

'They found him, Ashleigh, and he's going to be okay, they think. Battered and bruised, but alive.'

I cried then. I sobbed and sobbed and didn't care that each time I did, the pain in my ribs twisted like a knife. Dad just held my hand and let me get it all out.

The next thing I remember is waking up, the sun streaming through the windows and Mum and Dad slumped in a couple of chairs at my bedside. I tried not to wake them – they must have been up all night and completely exhausted – but almost as soon as I opened my eyes, Mum opened hers. Maybe being a parent gives you a sort of superpower in things like that. She smiled.

'Hey, sleeping beauty.'

'How's Aiden?' I said. 'Can I see him?'

'He's undergoing surgery,' Mum replied. She held up a hand, apparently in reaction to my expression. 'It's routine, Ash. He had a bit of a nasty head injury, but it's all going to be fine.'

Dad stretched and grimaced at some pain in his back.

'Morning, kiddlypunk,' he said.

'Don't you start,' I replied. 'Will I be able to see him when he's out of theatre?'

'He's not in this hospital, Ash,' said Dad. 'They took him to his normal clinic. They know his medical history there and he knows all the staff. It's for the best.'

'Why isn't anyone with him?'

'I'm going now,' said Mum. 'I just needed to make sure you were okay before I went. Don't worry, Ash, I'll be right there for him when he comes round.'

When Mum left, giving me a cautious hug that brought more tears to my eyes, Dad gave an update on all that had happened at the camp. What had hit me in the river was a mini tornado, a dust devil that had formed in a clearing in the bush close to the bank. He explained how it developed, something to do with hot air hitting a patch of cooler air forming a violent updraft. Once it crossed water it quickly lost power, but not before it had put me through a kind of watery tumble dryer.

'Mr Meredith said he'd never seen anything like it,' Dad said. 'And although your mum and I were thinking initially that the school must be at fault, I think now it was just a freak event. Like so many other freak weather events that have hit Australia for many years now. You just happened to be in the wrong place at the wrong time.'

Charlotte and Aiden were ahead of me when the mini tornado struck and it didn't affect them. But as soon as he saw I was in danger, Aiden dived into the water and followed me until we both slammed into the rocks that formed the rapids. When he was ripped from my grip he was bundled downstream, hitting his head a couple of times on the way. At some point, badly injured and probably barely conscious, he must have dragged himself to the river's edge and collapsed. The search party found him three kilometres downriver.

'He saved my life, Dad.' I could feel the tears starting to form again. 'He caught me.'

'Yes,' said Dad. He didn't say anything else and I was glad. There wasn't anything else to say. Dad poured me a glass of water and held it up as I sipped it through a straw.

'Dad,' I said.

'I'm here.'

'Can I ask a favour?'

'Go ahead.'

'Just before I was put on the helicopter, Mr Meredith told me about the man who got me off the rock and brought me to safety. His name is Mr Dyson and he has a son. Would you be able to find out where he lives?'

Dad frowned. 'I could ask the school, but they probably wouldn't tell me. Privacy concerns. But it shouldn't be too difficult. Why do you want to know?'

'I want you to send his son a present. A good present. Something he'd never be able to afford. Something like an expensive bike.'

Dad took my hand.

'A thankyou gift for what his father did for you.' It was a statement.

'No,' I replied. 'An apology. When you have it delivered, please put a card with it. "From two spoiled brats."'

Dad cocked his head to one side.

'Sounds like there's a story behind this.'

'There is,' I said. 'But it's not a story I want to tell right now.'

7

I was allowed to leave hospital two days later, with strict instructions to rest and allow my battered ribs to heal properly. As a result, Mum wouldn't let me visit Aiden, who was still recovering at his clinic. Even if I'd been in perfect physical shape, she probably wouldn't have allowed it. I'd been told that when he's getting his routine operations for Klinsmann's disease no one's allowed to visit because he's kept in isolation to minimise chances of infection. Not that I'd ever wanted to visit him then. Now I wasn't even allowed to call him. But Mum told me he was doing fine and would be home within the week, just in time for our birthday.

Mr Meredith and the class sent me a lovely big get-well card. All the school staff and my fellow students had signed it with personal messages. There was another card waiting for Aiden as well. The camp, it seemed, had been abandoned after the dust devil incident because too many students were worried about further accidents and no amount of reassurance that what had happened to me was freakishly improbable made those worries go away. So they'd all packed up the next day and come home. Apparently the school was arranging partial refunds to the parents.

I was going to be off school for a couple of weeks, but Mum said Charlotte could come to stay over around the time of our birthday, which was brilliant.

Resting is boring. I wasn't allowed to swim or even do much walking in the garden, so I spent a lot of time in the library. But even that paled after a while. And it's a funny thing. When I went to bed I'd find myself reaching across to take Aiden's hand. And when I found emptiness, I felt loneliness like a pain. Most nights I didn't sleep well at all.

I wasn't prepared for how Aiden would look when he finally came home. Dad brought him through the front door in a wheelchair and for the longest time, all I could do was stare. I'm not sure what I was expecting – the same old Aiden, I guess – but he was pale and obviously tired. The most dramatic thing was a contraption around his head that had metal spokes that seemed to dig straight into his skull; not that you could see much of his head, since it was wrapped in a bandage from just above his eyebrows. It was pretty obvious that Mum and Dad hadn't told me the whole story about just how ill Aiden had been. And perhaps still was. I forced myself to smile, though I felt more like crying.

'Hey, Aiden,' I said. 'Welcome home, bro.'

'Thanks,' he said. But he didn't smile and his voice seemed different somehow, as if that had been damaged as well.

I didn't know what else to say. I wanted to say thanks for saving my life, but that seemed weird somehow, there in our front room with Mum and Dad looking on. Artificial. So I just smiled. We'd talk later, probably in bed. I'd hold his hand and tell him how brave and wonderful he was. We had time.

'I'll take you to your room if you like, Aiden,' said Dad. 'You're probably a bit tired after the journey home, huh?'

'I'll take him, Dad,' I said.

'He's going to be in his own bedroom for a while, Ash,' said Mum. 'We've made up one of the spare rooms. It'll be better all round. Aiden will be sleeping upright for a while until the head brace comes off, and he gets restless at night. This way, you'll get a decent night's sleep and he won't be worried about disturbing you.'

'But I don't mind being disturbed,' I said. 'That's fine. We'll keep sharing a room, won't we, Aiden?'

He licked his lips, but even that simple act seemed to take a huge effort.

'I think I'd rather have my own space for a bit, Ashleigh,' he said. 'Just until I'm feeling a bit better.'

'Of course,' I said. 'Whatever you want.' But I have to admit, I felt a little hurt.

When Dad had wheeled him out of the room, Mum came over and put an arm around my shoulders.

'Just for a while, Ashleigh,' she said. 'He's been through a lot, you know. You both have. It's going to take a little time to get over this.'

I nodded.

'And I'll bring your birthday present home tomorrow,' she added. 'You're going to love it. Both of you.'

Our birthday was still two days away. She probably thought we needed a gift sooner rather than later, after all we'd been through.

'What is it?'

Mum ruffled my hair. 'Nice try, kiddlypunk,' she said. 'But I'll tell you this much. You are going to be surprised. Very surprised.'

I love surprises and most times, coming up to my birthday, I'd be so excited that I wouldn't be able to sleep. Lying in bed that night, though, I could only think about Aiden and what he was thinking and feeling a few doors down the corridor. He hadn't come out of the guest bedroom since Dad wheeled him in and Mum said I couldn't even go in to say goodnight. I tried some reading, but the words just floated off the page and didn't touch me. When I finally fell asleep, a thunderstorm rumbling, I had muddied dreams that gave me no rest whatsoever.

When I got down for breakfast Mum had already left for work. She often has the car pick her up at five-thirty in

92

the morning so she's in the lab by six o'clock. She says she likes the quiet at that time of the morning and it gives her space to think without the distraction of colleagues, questions and meetings. She gets her best ideas then, she says. I wasn't too bothered by that. I just wanted her to remember to bring our birthday present home, like she'd promised.

The weather had threatened a storm in the night, but it never arrived, just grumbled quietly way off in the distance. Now the sky was cloudless and even from inside the house I could tell it was going to be very hot. The kids at school wouldn't be getting out into the playground today, sunblock and hats regardless.

I made myself two rounds of toast and watched Dad clean the solar sail through the dining room window. It's meant to be self-cleaning, but Dad doesn't trust it. I would've knocked on the window to say good morning, but he was operating the pressure cleaner drone so there was no point. I took my breakfast into the library.

Aiden was already in there, which was a surprise. He was sitting in his wheelchair, staring at the shelves. Not reading, just staring. It's not often he seeks out time by himself. Normally he hangs around me whenever possible, only backing off when I tell him to give me some space. He didn't even turn around when I said good morning.

'How're you feeling, Aiden?' I asked.

He gripped the wheels of his chair and spun to face me. It was as if I'd surprised him, brought him back from somewhere far away in his head. He smiled.

'Oh, you know, Ash. Like my skull's on fire and someone's constantly stabbing me in the neck with a red-hot knife.'

'I'm sorry.'

'Don't be,' he said. 'I feel loads better than yesterday.'

I sat in one of the library reading chairs in front of him, put one hand on his knee. He glanced down as if surprised to see it there.

'Did they tell you what's wrong with you?' I asked. 'Why do you have to wear that cage thing and when's it coming off?'

'You know doctors, Ash,' he replied. Actually, I didn't. Until recently I hadn't needed any medical treatment, unlike Aiden who needed it constantly. 'They think you're an idiot who can't understand or handle the truth. So they just went on about head trauma, which means nothing at all really. Just that your head's been damaged and I could have told *them* that.' Aiden rarely talked about his medical experiences and he *never* made judgements about the doctors treating him. I felt a little uneasy. I mean, I know he was entitled to feel grumpy and maybe even angry at the injuries he'd got, but it's just that Aiden always... *accepted* what happened to him, rather than complaining about it. I didn't know whether to be pleased or worried that he was showing another side to his personality. 'The cage is to keep my head steady while it heals,' he continued. 'Stop my brain rattling around in there, or something. Mum says it's coming off in a few days and I'll also be able to get out of this chair. I hate being stuck in here, so that's good news for once.'

'I'm so sorry you've gone through all this, Aiden,' I said. 'And I want you to know how grateful I am that you risked your life to save mine. You've been amazingly brave.'

'Or amazingly dumb,' said Aiden. 'Depends on how you look at it.'

I put my head to one side. Another remark I never would have thought he'd make. But if anyone needed to have some slack cut for him, it was Aiden.

'What were you thinking about?' I said.

'When?'

'When I came in you were staring at the bookshelves and not like you were trying to decide what to read next. It seemed like you were thinking about something important.'

Aiden swung his wheelchair around and headed out the door towards the kitchen. I followed. I was going to offer to push him but almost instinctively knew that wouldn't be a good idea. Aiden was in a strange mood and I didn't think he'd like me interfering.

'The spider,' he said over his shoulder.

He wheeled himself to the fridge door, opened it and took out a flask of his green goo. Breakfast.

'What?'

He moved over to the kitchen table, unscrewed the flask and took a swig. I wanted to turn my eyes away, but forced myself to watch. He deserved that much respect.

'That golden orb-weaving spider we saw on camp,' he said.

'It was amazing. Mr Meredith told me not to let anyone else, other than you, know it was there. He said some of the other kids would destroy it, just because they could.'

'Probably right about that, our amazing, talented and empathetic teacher. But I was thinking it was symbolic of our family, Ash.'

'What?' This was getting weird.

'Think about it,' he said. 'The home the spider built was beautiful. She must have spent an enormous amount of time constructing it. An engineering marvel. Like this place.' He spread his arms wide. 'And there it is, in its environment, but if you didn't catch it at just the right angle, you'd never know it was there. Just like this place.'

'I don't know what you mean.'

'Oh, come on. All the security devices Mum must've installed. If someone was to come within half a kay of this beautiful mansion, alarms would go off. Not out there. In here. And before they knew it, someone trying to take anything from us – hell, even if they weren't thinking about it, but just stumbled across us accidentally – would be arrested or at least taken in by the security company Mum pays. It's like a web. Get too close and you're going to get stuck.'

'Aiden,' I said. 'That's just wrong. This house is not like that spider's web. It's beautiful, yeah, but it's not designed to trap anyone.'

'And then there's the female spider, right there in the centre of the web, controlling everything.' Aiden carried on as if I hadn't said anything. 'That's Mum right there. Huge, controlling, at the centre.' He laughed. 'And tiny, ineffectual Dad stuck at the edges, too scared to come close, never mind do anything.'

'I don't think you should talk about Mum and Dad like that, Aiden.' I was prepared to forgive him plenty of things after all he had done for me, but this was getting horrible. I wondered whether that head injury was much more severe than anyone had let on. But if that was the case, surely they wouldn't have allowed him to come home? I closed my eyes, forced myself to stay calm, reasonable and understanding.

Aiden didn't reply. He just sat there at the kitchen table, staring off into the distance. I'm not even sure he'd heard a word I'd said.

'And another thing,' he continued. 'We exist with no connection to the outside world. Not really. That spider's web was there, wonderful, rich and beautiful, but it was surrounded by the ugly. Battered, nasty nature, smashed to bits because of what we've done in the name of humanity, but if you look hard enough you'll find a gem in there, hiding away, pretending the ugliness doesn't exist.'

'Aiden...'

'People are suffering out there, Ashleigh, but we never see it. We stay in our beautiful web and *that's* our whole world. We're rich enough to make sure the real, ugly world is kept at a distance. So we can't be offended by it.'

I could feel tears coming to my eyes and I knew that if I didn't leave, then things would just become nastier. There was no talking to him and really I didn't want to listen to the nonsense he was coming out with. He needed rest, I told myself. In a few days he'd be back to normal.

But I didn't leave, because Dad opened the door from the outside and came in. He washed his hands at the sink.

'Hi, kids,' he said.

'Hey, Dad,' said Aiden. 'Got that solar sail gleaming?'

Dad smiled at us over his shoulder.

'Beautiful and at full efficiency,' he said. 'At least the half I've done today. I'll do the other half later, once I get dinner organised.'

'You could pay someone to do that,' said Aiden.

'Yes,' said Dad, drying his hands. 'But I enjoy it and what else am I going to do with my time?'

'Something useful?' said Aiden.

Dad gave us both a strange look at that. He sat slowly at the kitchen table and scratched his head.

'How about a video game?' he suggested after a long silence. 'If you guys have finished breakfast, I'm willing to kick your nearly-birthday bums at a game of your choice. You have been warned.'

'Sounds great, Dad,' said Aiden.

And the smile he gave appeared warm. And genuine.

'Oh, my God,' I said. 'Is that what I think it is?'

Mum placed the box down carefully on the kitchen table. There was a scuffling sound coming from it and the box rocked gently. It had air holes punched in its sides and a big red bow perched on the top.

'And how would I know what you think it is?' Mum replied. She smiled. 'You'll have to forgive me, Ashleigh, but my psychic powers are a bit off today.'

'It *is* what I think it is,' I said.

'Then you won't need to open the box,' said Dad. 'Let's put it away.' And he pretended to start doing just that.

I glanced at Aiden. He was looking a lot better now. He'd had a long sleep after we'd thrashed Dad at four different video games and his eyes were shining with excitement. It was almost unbearable for both of us. We wanted to open the box, but the anticipation was so delicious it seemed a shame to ruin it.

'You open it, Ashleigh,' said Aiden.

'No, you,' I replied. 'I'd like you to open it.'

So he did. He shouted with delight and put his hands into the box while I forced myself to be patient. In fact I even closed my eyes. I didn't know whether it was a cat or a dog, but I really wanted a dog. *Please make it a dog. Look, it's fine if it's a cat, but ...*

It gave the most adorable woof and I opened my eyes immediately. Love at first sight. Before first sight, really. The dog was small and furry and it had a little pug nose and its tail was wagging as if it was polishing the kitchen table and it was the most glorious, wonderful, fabulous, amazing birthday gift we'd ever got and I just had to hold it and stroke it and cuddle it and…

'It's gorgeous, Mum,' said Aiden. He looked up, eyes still shining, but immediately looked at the dog again, which sat on the table, tail still swirling, moving its head from side to side, and watching us with spheres of liquid brownness. I moved over next to Aiden and ran my hands through the dog's fur, scratched under its chin. It gazed up at me and I swear I saw love in those eyes.

'Is it real, Mum?' I said, voice all whispery and choked with emotion.

Mum laughed.

'Of course not, Ashleigh.' She sat at the table and ran her hand through the dog's fur. 'You know it's illegal to own pets.'

'Some people have real dogs,' said Aiden, but Mum held up her hand.

'I know, Aiden, but they're breaking the law and we won't ever do that. No. This is better than real. This won't get sick and it won't die. At least I don't think it will.'

'You made it,' I said.

'Oh, yeah,' said Mum. 'It's state-of-the-art.' She gently opened the dog's mouth, exposing a pink tongue and a set of small teeth. When she let go, the dog sneezed and we all laughed. 'Based on some AI devices I'd already engineered for work in dangerous environments. War zones, places like that. Though we have sold or given away a number to blind people for use as guide dogs. But matey here is different.'

'Why?' Aiden and I asked together.

'Because those dogs were nothing like as realistic,' said Mum. 'They didn't have to be because basically they were designed for functionality, rather than aesthetics.'

I opened my mouth to ask, but Mum beat me to it.

'They were meant to work, rather than look good,' she said. 'For the guide dogs, I put fur on them and gave them the ability to lick their owners. Sometimes it's important for a machine to give the impression of friendship – love, even – and some blind people need all the love they can get. But your dog... well, he can do things that the others simply can't.'

'Like?' prompted Aiden.

'He can learn. He has the new generation of artificial intelligence algorithms installed and this means that, basically, he interacts with his environment, learns from it and changes behaviour accordingly.' Mum was in full lecture mode now. 'A machine will keep getting burned if it strays into a fire. A proper AI machine will do that maybe a couple of times, but then it will learn to recognise that fire is unpleasant and avoid it. In many ways, the principle is exactly the same as the way babies learn about the world. This dog will just do it a lot quicker.' Mum ruffled the dog's head and it stood up on its four stubby little legs. 'Try getting it to sit,' Mum said.

I looked at Aiden and he looked at me. He nodded, giving me permission.

'Sit,' I said. The dog cocked its head to one side, regarded me. But it stayed standing. I tried again, this time, putting gentle pressure on its back, close to the tail.

'Sit,' I said. The dog yawned and walked off. Aiden and I laughed.

'You're going to have to teach it,' said Mum. 'It will learn, trust me. It'll sit, roll over, play dead, come to heel, do everything a real dog can do. It's just going to take time.'

'Could we teach it to talk?' asked Aiden. There was silence for a couple of beats and then I burst out laughing. But I was the only one. 'If it's AI, then it shouldn't be restricted just to things a dog can do,' he continued. 'It could learn anything. How to play chess, how to paint, how to talk.'

Mum rested her chin on her interlocked fingers.

'That's true, up to a point, Aiden,' she said. 'But it does depend on the programming and, most importantly, physical design. This dog does not have opposable thumbs, so it's going to have real difficulty moving a chess piece, let alone picking up a paintbrush. Its vocal cords and all the physical stuff associated with sounds are based on a dog's anatomy, so it won't be able to speak, even if it becomes super-smart.' She smiled. 'I made you a dog. If you want to play chess and talk, that's what your sister's for. She's just not as cute and adorable.'

'Ha, ha,' I said. 'Anyway, I don't want this dog to talk. I want it to be a dog.'

Mum told us a number of other things about our present, like how it would find a patch of sun when its energy levels started to fall, so that it could recharge. I picked him up from the table and placed him carefully on the floor. He licked my hand and I nearly died with pleasure.

'What's his name?' I asked.

'It's your present,' Mum said. 'You and Aiden will have to work that out between you.'

'Was it expensive to make?' asked Aiden.

Mum pursed her lips and shook her head.

'I'm not saying,' she replied. 'Not because I don't want to tell you – and I do know, down to the dollar, how much Fido here cost to manufacture.' She paused. 'I just don't want to say the figures out loud. They'd scare your father half to death and I know this because they sure as hell scare the living daylights out of me.'

That was fine by me. I didn't care.

You couldn't put a price on this present.

8

'Oh, my God,' said Charlotte. 'He's adorable. What's his name?'

'Zorro,' I said. 'Z for short.'

'That's a strange name.'

Aiden had suggested it. He pointed out that the dog had a dark patch over both eyes and there was a kind of zigzag pattern on his back where black fur was mottled in with grey. According to Aiden, Zorro was a really old fictional character, a bit like a superhero. He always wore a mask and he'd slash a 'Z' into things with a sword, like a sort of old-time tag. So Zorro it was.

It had only taken the dog a day to learn the sound of his name and it was incredibly cute when he jumped up and looked at you. He was also sitting on command, though sometimes he wouldn't bother if he didn't feel like it. I thought that was brilliant and just the way a real dog would behave. I didn't *always* feel like doing what I was told, so why should a dog?

'How does he get his power?' asked Charlotte.

'You see his fur? Each strand is a tiny fibre optic cable. All together they act like about a zillion solar panels.'

Charlotte was jealous, and who wouldn't be? Normally, I'd be happy that she was jealous of what I had, but for some reason that didn't seem as important today. This was the first time I'd seen her in person since camp, though we'd video-called each other heaps. On one of those occasions I asked her what had happened to our official complaint against Mr Dyson. She said she'd had a bit of a rethink after he dived in to save me when I was lashed to the rock, and she didn't like to ask Mr Meredith what had happened. I was pretty sure Mr M hadn't done anything about it and it wasn't difficult to get Charlotte to agree to forget the whole thing. I felt loads better when she did.

I took Z into the pool room with us, partly to show off, I guess, but mainly because he *was* so adorable. He'd spent two nights curled up on Aiden's bed, and after all Aiden had been through I couldn't bring myself to ask for my share of the dog's night-time company. Anyway, I was still hoping Aiden would come back to our room when he was feeling a little better. Then Z could sleep between us.

Mum had said I could swim, provided I didn't 'overdo it' and she'd also said there was no reason why Zorro couldn't either.

'Totally waterproof,' she said. 'To at least one hundred metres. Beyond that, I wouldn't risk it.'

So the dog ran up and down the side of the pool while Charlotte and I drifted and floated and swam. Z occasionally gave a small yip as if he wanted to join us and was just waiting for permission.

'Well, come on then,' I said, clapping my hands. 'Jump in, you goober.'

And he did. It was amazing. One moment the dog was turning in tight circles, the next he had launched himself straight into the pool. Charlotte and I shrieked with laughter as he hit the surface.

I stopped laughing when he sank like a stone.

'Oh, my God.' I said and duck-dived immediately. Z had gone off into the deep end, naturally, so it was a bit of an effort to make it down to the bottom of the pool. When I got there, he was sitting on the floor tiles looking up at me; it was so funny I nearly burst out laughing, which is probably not the wisest thing to do when you're on the bottom of a swimming pool. I managed to get to the surface, spluttering and choking, holding a wet dog that was as heavy as a brick. I placed him on the edge of the pool and he just stood there, dripping and blinking.

'Shake yourself,' I said. 'That's what wet dogs do. They shake themselves.'

But he drip-dried instead, while Charlotte and I nearly died laughing. I guessed Zorro was going to be relying on me and Aiden for a lot of training over the coming months. I was putting my hand up for swim instructor.

Our birthday dinner was terrific. Dad had gone to town on a cake that was shaped like a dog. It even had Zorro's markings in icing on the side and thirteen candles along its spine. Aiden and I blew the candles out and Dad cut slices of cake for me, Charlotte and himself. Mum was at work and wouldn't be back until late, if at all. Sometimes she slept at the office.

Aiden watched us eat. I don't know how he does it every year. The cakes are yummy. But I guess it's what you get used to. Then Charlotte gave us our presents. She'd got us the same thing, which I suppose is sensible – a hologram app for our tablets. We already had one of those installed, but it had bugs and the hologram it generated of whoever you were talking to was grainy and disappeared at odd moments. This app was terrific. I took my tablet into my room and called Dad, who was, of course, still in the kitchen cleaning up. As soon as he answered, this miniature Dad appeared on my bedclothes. Really lifelike and so solid-looking that I felt this irresistible urge to poke him in the stomach to see if I could make him fall over. I couldn't. My finger disappeared into the hologram instead. It was brilliant fun.

Charlotte and I talked until nearly midnight. About school and what had been happening since I'd been away (not much, it seemed), but mainly about camp. The kids were bummed that it had all been called off, even though they were the ones who had insisted because they were scared. Charlotte was annoyed that she'd missed out on the horseriding.

'I've always wanted to ride a horse,' she said. 'When I got back from camp, I made Mum and Dad promise they'd take me. There's a pony club on the other side of Sydney, apparently, but it's really expensive and there's a waiting list to join. Dad's taking me to see it next Monday after school. Perhaps you'd like to come along too, Ash. Then you could sleep over at my place, if you want.'

'Sure,' I said. Actually, I wasn't sure about the horse business. I'd kinda changed my mind about it being an ambition. From the movies I'd seen, being perched on top of a horse just meant you had a long way to fall and the landing was always going to be hard. Plus, they appeared to be dangerous at both ends. I'd think about it.

'My house is nothing like as nice as yours, though,' Charlotte added. Her mouth twisted as if she regretted inviting me. I knew what she was thinking. No house could match up to mine and she was worried she'd be embarrassed. 'I mean, we don't have a pool or anything, and ...'

'I'm sure it will be lovely,' I replied. I wasn't sure, of course, but Charlotte smiled and relaxed, which was the main thing.

We giggled, we gossiped, we chatted.

Eventually, we fell asleep, our words slurring and blurring into nothing.

I have no idea why I woke at two-thirty in the morning. Maybe a sound startled me, though as I lay in the darkness listening, I couldn't hear anything at all. I strained my ears but there weren't even the normal sounds of a house creaking and groaning as the cooler night air made the building bend and twist.

Then Charlotte farted in her sleep.

It wasn't very loud, but it was high-pitched, and I knew that I was going to burst out laughing. So I hopped out of bed, bottling up my laughter as best I could – it was a real strain, and I knew I'd have to let it out soon because the pressure was building. Then I thought that was probably what had caused Charlotte to fart in the first place, which only made things worse. I could feel the laughter coming down my nose, but I made it out of my bedroom, shutting the door before letting out a yelp that was almost hysterical.

There was a light on in Aiden's room and I tapped gently on his door when I'd recovered a bit, but there was no reply. Maybe he'd fallen asleep with the light on. I thought it would be a good idea to sneak in and turn it off. Mum and Dad were always going on about conserving energy, even though we generated huge amounts through our solar sail and stored it in a massive array of batteries. But, to be honest, that was just an excuse. I knew Z was in there, lying on Aiden's bed, and I couldn't resist the opportunity to give him a cuddle.

Aiden was awake and sitting in the wheelchair, with that strange contraption still framing his skull. He was due to go into the clinic in the morning to have it removed. He'd also been promised that he could leave the chair behind and walk to the waiting car when all procedures had been done. I could only imagine how much he was looking forward to that. His eyes were open and fixed on the wall. He didn't even turn his gaze to me when I came into the room.

'Hey, Aiden,' I said. He slowly moved his entire head to face me and smiled, though that was small and faded almost immediately. 'Can't you sleep?' I continued.

'I've been thinking,' he replied.

I sat down on the edge of his bed. Zorro stirred and uncurled himself from a pile of Aiden's pillows. I ran a hand through his fur and he rolled onto his back. I knew Aiden had been teaching him about belly-rubbing.

'What about?'

'All sorts of things,' he replied.

'Give me an example.'

'Is it possible to love a machine?'

'What?'

He scratched himself under his right eye. He had to do it carefully because of the framework.

'Your tablet with its new whizzy app. Would you say you love that?'

It was a strange question, so I didn't reply right away. If Aiden had been spending hours thinking about this, then he wouldn't be happy with an answer straight off the top of my head.

'I do love it,' I said finally. 'It makes me happy, and if it can give me that emotion, then why shouldn't it loveable?'

'As loveable as Mum and Dad? As loveable as me?'

'No,' I said. 'Of course not. We're all related, obviously. Flesh and blood. My tablet isn't.'

'But that's the point I'm making,' said Aiden. He was really animated now, as if I'd touched on something crucial. 'Why is flesh and blood so important?'

I rubbed at my forehead and tried to frame an argument, but it didn't matter because Aiden was in full flow now.

'I can say that I love Zorro already,' he said. 'He's cute and loyal and funny and...well, just fantastic. But he's a machine. Really, when it comes down to it, he's just an assembly of wires and conductors and algorithms. I can't love a wire by itself or a conductor and I certainly can't love an algorithm, but when you put them all together like Mum has done with Zorro, then I love the whole. So why don't I love a solar sail?'

'Because it doesn't seem alive.'

'Exactly.' Aiden was so enthusiastic, I felt strangely pleased, like I'd given a teacher the right answer in a particularly tough test. 'The appearance of being alive. I've been thinking about Turing.'

'Who?'

'Alan Turing. Look him up on your tablet. He's a really old computer guy, one of the first to even think about computers. He came up with a test to determine whether machines can actually think.' Aiden stared off into the distance as if marshalling his memories and arranging his thoughts. I waited. 'He proposed a kind of game. Have one person, the tester, in a room with a computer that's connected to two other rooms, each with computers. In one of the rooms is a person, but in the other room there's just the computer and the code that works it. Now have the tester ask questions of the other two rooms. In one, a person will type in their response; in the other the computer will do it. What does it mean if the tester can't tell what is a human response and what is a machine's response, no matter how many questions he asks?'

I tried thinking this through, but it was difficult.

'It doesn't mean the computer can think,' I said finally. 'It just means the computer can imitate a person really well.'

'But if it can imitate it so well that no one can ever tell the difference, it *becomes* human, doesn't it?'

'Errr…'

'Or maybe people's minds are really just like exceptionally sophisticated computers that are programmed to produce emotions like love. That would work, wouldn't it? We'd all be asking the wrong question. It's not, "Can machines become human?" but "Are humans really just another type of machine?" If so, then we can love machines and they can love us back. They'd be alive, just as we are alive. Of course, then there's John Searle and the Chinese Room thought experiment…'

I held up a hand.

'Aiden,' I said. 'My brain, the computer in my head, whatever, is hurting right now. And it's really tired. Tell me about it some other time. I'm going back to bed.' I scuffed Zorro under the chin and he licked my hand. 'Love you, puppy,' I said. 'And you, bro,' I said to Aiden.

He laughed.

When I got to the door, he spoke once more.

'Another thing I've been thinking about, Ash,' he said. 'That girl in the park. Xena.'

'What about her?'

'I want to talk to her again.'

That stopped me. I'd been thinking about her on and off as well and as soon as Aiden said he wanted to speak to her, I realised that was something I wanted too. But it was impossible, so I'd never allowed the wish to properly form.

'Why?'

'Because I think she might have answers to other questions I need answered.'

'Like what?'

But Aiden was back inside his own head and I don't think he even heard me.

Aiden was in the clinic most of the following day, but when he got back he seemed much happier. The frame was gone and he was walking, though I think I detected a very slight limp in his right leg. Dad agreed that we could both go swimming, though he put a one-hour limit on it. More importantly, he told us that he and Mum were agreed that we could both go back to school on Monday. That gave us just three more days of being cooped up in the house.

Z improved slightly at swimming. Aiden and I took it in turns to hold him in the water, one hand under his belly, and get him to make walking movements. When all four legs were going, we'd let go and he would swim maybe a couple of metres before he'd stop and sink like a brick. Aiden dived and got him each time. I struggled to dive that deep, whereas my brother made it look easy.

We rested at the side of the pool. Dad seemed to have forgotten the hour rule and we weren't going to remind him. I put my arm around Aiden's shoulders.

'Are you ready to move back into our bedroom?' I asked.

'Not really,' he said. There was no hesitation. He kicked away from the wall and floated on his back a metre away, staring at the ceiling. 'I like having my own room. It feels like a place I don't have to share. I asked Mum and Dad and they said I could stay where I am.' He scissored up to face me, treading water. 'No offence, Ash. And anyway, you've always moaned about having me in there. Plus, let's be honest. We're both thirteen now. It's not like we're kids afraid of the dark.'

'You're right,' I said, as breezily as I could manage. 'Way too old to be sharing a room.' I splashed him in the face. 'I don't even like you,' I added.

'You said you *loved* me last night.'

'That's when you were sick and stuck in that wheelchair. I felt sorry for you.'

He splashed me back and that started a proper water war, which got us both laughing.

So why was it that I felt a little sad when I thought about going to bed that night?

9

The class gave us a round of applause when we entered the classroom the following Monday. This time I didn't feel embarrassed at being the centre of attention. I even gave a small bow before sitting down next to Charlotte.

'Welcome back,' said Mr Meredith. 'We've missed you, Ashleigh and Aiden Delatour, and we're thrilled you have returned to the fold. If you see me at recess, I will let you know the work you've missed. Now.' He clapped his hands together. 'Time, class, to learn about the Great European Famine of Thirty-Two. Please make notes on your tablets and pay attention...'

Charlotte's father picked us up after school. Dad came for Aiden and, as arranged, handed over a small case with pyjamas and toiletries in it for me. I was excited about having a sleepover at Charlotte's house – I mean, home was great, but occasionally I longed for something different. I wondered if that was why I'd been thinking about Xena recently.

Charlotte's dad was small and full of nervous energy. He shook my hand as he introduced himself, but couldn't maintain eye contact for more than a second. His gaze flitted everywhere, as if he was afraid of missing something or someone more important. His hand was slightly clammy and when he let go of mine, I wiped it on the back of my dress.

We hadn't been driving for more than a minute when he gave Charlotte the news.

'I'm afraid we'll have to postpone the visit to the riding club,' he said over his shoulder. 'Something's come up.'

'Oh, Dad!' said Charlotte. 'You promised.'

'I know. I know.' His fingers tapped on the steering wheel. 'One of my men rang in sick and we have a function this afternoon. An important function. I've got to go in his place.'

'But...'

'Charlotte, we cannot afford...' His voice was firm and he glanced at us in the rear-view mirror. When he spoke again his tone was calmer. 'We'll talk about this later. Okay? I meant what I said. The contacts there could be very useful. And I promise we will go at some time. Just not tonight.' His eyes skidded over mine for a moment. 'I'm sorry to disappoint you, Ashleigh.'

'Not a problem,' I replied. 'I'm just happy to hang out with Charlotte.' It was true, but I'm not sure he believed me because he promised I'd be invited to the reorganised trip. Charlotte squeezed my hand as if sympathising with my disappointment. I didn't tell her it was non-existent.

The journey to Charlotte's house took a little over twenty minutes, through an area of Sydney I hadn't seen before. Some of it was fire-ravaged, swathes of houses and parklands charred and bleak in the afternoon sun. It was depressing and I was glad when the housing estate appeared, as if offering refuge, in the distance. Charlotte's father pressed a button on the dashboard of the car and a gate in the estate's wall opened up as we approached, then closed behind us.

The estate itself was neat, ordered and obviously well-maintained. Front gardens were nicely manicured and a few people walked the streets. They waved at the car as we passed. Charlotte's house was somewhere near the middle of the estate and it was much bigger than other houses we'd passed. It was also different in that it was fenced in its own grounds. Once again, Charlotte's father pressed a button and part of the fencing slid back to let the car in.

'Welcome to my home,' said Charlotte.

'It's great,' I said. It was detached and had clearly been extended. I thought I could see a glass conservatory to one side of the building, but it became lost to view as we drove up to the front door. The car doors swung open and Charlotte and I got out.

'I'll be back for dinner,' said Charlotte's father through the driver's window. 'Eight o'clock sharp, Charlotte.'

'Okay.'

'And remember what I said about making up for lost time. You hear me?'

'Sure, Dad,' Charlotte called back.

And the car drove back the way we'd come.

'Your father works a lot?' I asked.

Charlotte's mouth twisted. 'A lot? No. He works all the time. *All* the time. Even when he's home he's working. He works in his sleep.'

I laughed, but Charlotte didn't even smile.

Her bedroom was small, but nicely decorated. A queen-sized bed faced the lone window and there was a couch against one wall. Charlotte had already warned me we'd be sharing the bed and I was cool with that. Provided she didn't fart.

Most of the room was obviously dedicated to study. A huge desk took up the longest wall and on it were writing materials and a handful of old books, as well as a standalone tablet built into the wall. Above the tablet was a huge sign.

Winners embrace hard work. Losers see it as punishment. And that's the difference. Underneath the words was the name Lou Holtz.

'Who's he?' I asked Charlotte.

'A twentieth-century sporting icon. He specialised in motivational quotes.'

I tried to look impressed, but I'm not sure I succeeded.

'I really like your room,' I said. And I did, too. Mine was about three times the size and my bed was much bigger as well, but her room was...cosy.

I lay down on the bed and Charlotte took the couch. I put my hands behind my head and examined another sign on the ceiling above me. *The best way to predict your future is to create it*. That, apparently, was by someone called Abraham Lincoln. What was it with signs in this household? I thought about asking Charlotte, but then decided to give it a pass.

'I'm a bit worried about Aiden,' I said.

'Why?'

I explained how Aiden had been acting strange recently. That he spent more time on his own and much of that time he was staring into space. Thinking, apparently. I gave her a quick rundown of the strange conversation we'd had in his bedroom the night Charlotte stayed over. What I didn't say was that I was concerned his focus no longer seemed to be exclusively on me, but rather in the private world of his own mind. True, I'd often complained that he was *too* attentive. Now I was bothered that he wasn't attentive enough. Maybe I should do some of my own thinking, take a long, hard look at myself in the process.

'Puberty,' said Charlotte when I was done.

'What?'

'Puberty,' she said again. 'Don't tell me you don't know what puberty means, Ashleigh.'

Of course I knew what puberty meant. It was just that I'd never thought of applying it to me or anyone else. Maybe I'd just assumed Aiden and I would stay kids forever.

'It's the start of the process whereby both girls and boys prepare for parenthood, turning from kids to adults...'

'Yeah, Charlotte, I know...' But I might as well have been trying to stop a runaway truck with an outstretched hand.

'It all starts with gonadotropin-releasing hormones, which the hypothalamus secretes at the start of puberty. When that GnRH hits the pituitary gland, a pea-sized organ in the brain, then – bang – the chain reaction starts.'

'Yes...'

'Two more hormones are released in both males and females – luteinising hormone and follicle-stimulating hormone and these go to work on the body. In a boy they go to the testes...'

'Please, Charlotte...'

'...where they produce testosterone. In girls, however, they target the ovaries and produce oestrogen. Of course, all of this produces some dramatic changes in the bodies of both sexes.'

'How do you know all this stuff, Charlotte? You're like a walking textbook.' I wasn't going to stop her by conventional means, so I thought I'd appeal to her vanity. It worked.

'I study,' said Charlotte. She pointed to the sign above my head. 'That's the only way to create my future.'

'Right,' I said. I thought that maybe other things were more vital. Food and drink, for example. Breathing. But I decided to keep those thoughts to myself. 'So you reckon these hormones are messing with Aiden's head? That he's started puberty?'

'That's my diagnosis,' said Charlotte with what seemed like considerable satisfaction. 'Hormones play havoc with emotions as well as bodily functions. We could get moody or depressed, become entirely unpredictable. Often parents think their kid has turned into some kind of monster...'

I zoned out then. Aiden had started puberty? It made sense, though happening pretty much bang on our thirteenth birthday seemed a coincidence. I thought about my own feelings, did a mental check of my body, but I couldn't really detect any changes. Maybe my – what had Charlotte called it? GBH or some acronym? Maybe that hormone was on its way to my bits and I'd wake up tomorrow all hairy and grumpy. It was a disturbing thought.

Charlotte's father didn't turn up to dinner. In fact, I didn't see him until the following morning when he drove us to school. So that evening, at eight o'clock sharp, we ate a limp salad with obviously fake chicken slices by ourselves. Her mother didn't join us either. She put the food out on plates in front of us, smiled at me nervously and then bustled off somewhere. I was beginning to realise that in Charlotte's household everyone was busy all the time. Maybe Charlotte's comment about her dad wasn't a joke. Maybe they *did* all work in their sleep.

I brought up the subject later that night when we were lying in bed, waiting for sleep but trying to put it off at the same time. I hadn't heard the car come back and Charlotte's bedroom was just above the front door.

'What's your dad's job, Charlotte?'

'He's a security manager,' she replied. 'This community. Most of the families here work for Dad. That's why we've got the nicest house in the place. He employs hundreds of people, some who are responsible for keeping this community safe, but others who are hired out for special functions.' She yawned and I couldn't blame her. The conversation *was* a bit boring. 'That's where he must be now. I don't know. I don't ask much about his work.'

'Does this community need to be kept safe?'

Charlotte rolled onto her side, put her cheek on her hand and regarded me as if I'd lost my mind.

'Of course,' she replied. 'That's why there's a wall around the perimeter. To keep us in and others out. It's one of the reasons our house is the most secure here. The closer you live to the wall, the more chance there is of being attacked by anyone getting over or through it. That's why it's guarded twenty-four seven. Come on, Ash. You must know *something* about security. What protections are in place at your house?'

I shrugged. Aiden had had plenty to say on the subject, but it wasn't something I'd paid any attention to. It wasn't something I'd *needed* to pay attention to.

'My dad might have been the one who installed whatever security you have. He's an expert in this sort of stuff. But whatever you have, it must be pretty sophisticated. The fact there's no wall around your house tells me that.'

Now *I* yawned. I could feel sleep sneaking up on me. Before it could claim me, one small niggle at the back of my mind demanded attention.

'Charlotte?'

'Hmmm?' Sleep was stalking her as well.

'Your dad said something about you making up lost time. When he dropped us off. What did he mean? Just tell me if it's none of my business…'

'Oh that. That's about the time I'm spending with you, Ash.'

'What do you mean?'

'This is time I could spend studying. I *should* spend studying. So Mum and Dad made me agree that I would make up the time wasted today by studying extra for the rest of the week.'

I gave that some thought. Wasted time? I didn't understand. How could relaxation with a friend be wasted time?

'I have a schedule for studying,' she continued. 'A certain number of hours per week. If I don't do any tonight, I'll have to make it up later, even if I have to work through the night. It's non-negotiable.'

'I don't understand.'

'You're rich, Ashleigh Delatour. Your mother and father will provide for you for the rest of your life. But most of us can't bank on that. Mum and Dad work twenty-four seven, but that barely covers the cost of this place and educational fees. They sacrifice a huge amount just to keep me at school, even though I won a scholarship that pays three-quarters of the fees. The least I can do is work as hard as I can to provide for the future. One day I will be as rich and as powerful as your mother. Because, as the sign says, I'll create my future. No one else will.'

I didn't know what to say so I said nothing. After a few minutes I heard Charlotte's breathing fall into the rhythm of sleep. I tried to follow suit, but there were so many thoughts going around in my head. I'd assumed so much. I'd assumed Charlotte was naturally smart and possessed of a brilliant memory. It hadn't occurred to me that maybe she was forced to spend countless hours alone in this room just to give that impression. I'd assumed her parents were wealthy – not as wealthy as mine, naturally – but wealthy all the same. How else could they have afforded to send her on that ill-fated camp? I realised I had no proper understanding of how the world operated. Maybe Aiden was right. Maybe the Delatour family was determined to keep the ugly world at a distance so we couldn't be offended by it.

I eventually fell asleep, but my dreams were fractured and restless.

I was woken by a siren in the middle of the night. It made me jolt upright in bed, my heart hammering. Charlotte barely stirred. Her eyes flickered open and she put a hand on my arm.

'It's okay,' she mumbled. 'Go back to sleep.'

'What is it?'

'Just an alarm from the wall. Happens all the time. Dad and his men will sort it. Go back to sleep.'

But I couldn't. Even when the noise stopped, about half an hour later, I couldn't. I stared at the dark space above the bed, listened to the silence and waited until morning slowly bathed the room in light.

Charlotte's theory about puberty explaining Aiden's mood swings and strange behaviour had stayed with me. I tried to tackle him about it the following day, after dinner (it featured chips – Mum was away on yet another conference).

'Do you feel all grumpy, Aiden? Maybe a bit depressed? Feeling like you aren't in control of your own body?'

'Your face is all grumpy,' he said. And smiled. This was something we'd seen in an old movie. This character kept saying 'your face' when replying to a question. It was really stupid and childish and we'd stopped doing it ourselves a year or so ago. We'd just forgotten about it. I was amazed – and curiously pleased – that it seemed to have made a reappearance.

'I'm serious,' I said.

'Your face is serious,' said Aiden. 'And your face is depressed.'

'It is now I'm talking to you.'

'Ha, ha, good one, Ash-face.'

'Your face is an ash-face,' I said and we both cracked up laughing at that.

So he never did confirm Charlotte's diagnosis, but the fact that he was in such a good and talkative mood seemed to indicate she was on the right track. He'd been so *intense* the night before last. Scarily so. I could almost hear those hormones racing through his body.

I felt both of us were in for a tough time of it for the next couple of years.

Turns out I didn't know the half of it.

I heard Mum and Dad arguing on their video-call later that evening. Aiden and I had gone to the pool, but I'd got out to use the bathroom and it was as I was going back that I heard Dad's voice in the kitchen. I don't know why I stopped. I wouldn't normally listen in to my parents' conversation – mainly because it would be *really* boring – but for some reason, maybe the tone in Dad's voice, I stopped by the door and peeked in. He had his back to me and he was staring down at the tablet in his hand. I took a step or two to one side. I didn't want Mum to see me appear in the corner of her screen.

'I understand why you have to be away so often, Chrissie. I do,' said Dad. 'The work you do is incredibly important and you know I've always been totally supportive…'

'So what's changed now?' Mum's voice was a bit tinny and there was a slight echo to it, but she was in New Delhi, so the reception probably wasn't as good as normal.

'Nothing's changed. It's just that Ashleigh's getting older, becoming more independent and I think I really need to take a look at *my* life, what I've achieved or what I *could* achieve, before it's too late.'

'You've always been happy to stay at home...'

'Yeah, I've loved it. Seriously loved it. But when you get old, Chrissie, you'll be able to look back on a life that's accomplished so much, done so much good in the world, whereas I...well, I'm not saying being a stay-at-home dad isn't valuable. I know it is. But I'm not sure I'm needed anymore. Maybe it's time to...I don't know, *do* something.'

'Is this a mid-life crisis, Gareth?'

'Oh, for God's sake...' Dad put a hand to his head and the tablet to his chest. He took a deep breath and lifted the device up once more. 'All I'm saying is that when the kids are at school I could do something that, in only a small way, maybe, would help. I dunno. Maybe volunteer work at the food kitchens for the poor, that kind of thing. Help out with renewal of vegetation. Or give free classes on vegetable production to those in need. And, if all that goes well, maybe doing something like that full-time. We could employ a nanny or something, give work to a person who probably desperately needs it. God knows we've got the money to do it.'

There was silence at Mum's end for a few seconds.

'Let's talk about this when I get home, Gareth,' she said. 'I didn't know you were unhappy with your life and of course you should do something if you feel it has no meaning. Gotta go. Talk later. Bye.'

'I'm not *saying* my life has no meaning, Chrissie...' But she was gone. Dad stared at the screen for a moment or two and then put his tablet down on the kitchen table. He put it down with more force that I thought was strictly necessary. I suddenly realised that if he turned now, he'd catch me eavesdropping, so I tiptoed past the door and back to the pool room.

I could only hope that he didn't notice the puddle of water I'd left outside the door or, if he did, that he wouldn't put two and two together.

I got to have Zorro in my bed that night. It was the first time he'd slept with me.

I plumped up a pillow for him and he lay there, staring at me as I tickled him behind the ear. But after about twenty minutes he jumped off the bed and padded over to the closed door, where he sat and whined.

'What is it, Z?' I asked. 'Can't be needing a wee, because you don't *do* wees, do you?' Maybe I'd ask Mum if she could program that into him. It would make him even more realistic and I'd be happy to clean up any mistakes he might do around the house.

The dog kept whining, so eventually I got up and opened my door. He immediately trotted down the corridor and squeezed into Aiden's bedroom. A few moments later, the door closed.

I felt like crying. And I also felt that somehow it was my own fault. The dog was learning things very quickly, and obviously Aiden had been teaching him loyalty. Not loyalty to *us*, but loyalty to Aiden. I found it hard to believe that he had left his bedroom door open out of carelessness. I'd been *nice*, letting Aiden have Z in his room all the time. Now I felt my generosity had been used against me. The trouble was, I didn't know what to do about it. I couldn't get resentful at the person who'd saved my life. That would make me a total bitch. So I went back to my bedroom, picked up my book and tried to pretend I wasn't hurting.

I'd only been thirteen a few days, but in that time, my brother was getting weird, probably because of hormones that were almost certainly heading my way, my mum was halfway round the planet, my dad was unhappy looking after us, maybe resenting us, and my dog didn't like me. Okay, maybe he *did* like me, but not nearly as much as he liked Aiden. And my best friend was a know-it-all who tried to make me feel stupid. Who *did* make me feel stupid.

It was self-pity. I knew that. But sometimes a bit of self-pity can be just what you need. So I sobbed myself to sleep at the injustice of how the world treated Ashleigh Delatour and in the morning I felt loads better.

10

'I'm going over the fence at lunchtime,' said Aiden.

'You're doing what?'

'I want to talk to Xena. Are you coming with me?'

'You're nuts, Aiden. Of course I'm not coming with you. Have you forgotten the trouble we got into last time? Get caught again and Mum and Dad'll kill us.'

'They won't kill us.'

'No, they won't kill us. They'll just make us wish they had. It's crazy, Aiden. Don't do it.'

'Hey, that's fine if you want to stay, Ash. Probably better, really. If I get caught, then it'll only be me in trouble.'

'You're not going.'

'I am.'

'What makes you think she'd even be there? Just because she was at that park once at lunchtime, doesn't mean she's there *every* lunchtime. You need to grow up.'

'Yeah, well. Only one way to find out.'

'I forbid it.' I thought about crossing my arms, like Mum does when she's being particularly fierce, but I wouldn't have been able to take myself seriously.

'Good luck with that,' said Aiden.

'I'll tell Mr Meredith.'

'No, you won't.'

And he was right. I wouldn't. I didn't. Instead I watched as he scaled the fence at lunchtime and disappeared down Albert Street. I couldn't even stand there peering through the fence and waiting for him to come back, because that would have made someone on yard duty suspicious, so I just strolled around the grounds, trying to be cool but actually churning with worry. Now I wished I *had* gone with him. It would've been better than waiting here, nursing an overactive imagination.

He was gone twenty minutes. I saw him approaching the fence out of the corner of my eye as I was talking to the teacher on yard duty.

'Ow,' I said, blinking furiously. 'I think I've got something in my eye, Miss. Could you look, please?'

She tilted my head up and I held open my eyelid as best I could. Apparently she couldn't find anything, which didn't come as a great surprise to me. I blinked a couple more times, announced myself cured and thanked her. Aiden strolled past, hands in pockets, whistling. I caught up with him.

'Well?' I hissed.

'Never better, thanks,' he said. 'You?'

And it was then I noticed the small cut above his right eye. I pointed it out to him.

'Ah, yes,' he said. 'That's where my head came into contact with a kid's knuckles. Bit unfortunate.' He held up his right hand, made a fist. There were scrapes along its back. 'Which is when these came into contact with *his* head.'

'My God, Aiden,' I said. 'You've been in a *fight*?'

'Not a lot gets past you, does it, Ash? What gave you the first clue?'

I grabbed him by the sleeve, pulled him further away from a group of girls huddled together, chatting and laughing.

'You've just recovered from a serious head injury, Aiden,' I pointed out. 'And you get into a fight? Are you crazy?'

He laughed. 'I'm beginning to think so. Settle down, Ash. It's nothing. You should see the other guy. He's not looking as pretty as me.'

I sighed. 'I don't know what's got into you recently, Aiden,' I said. 'I reckon that injury to your head has addled your brains.' But he just kept grinning. 'So was all that worth it?' I added. 'Did you see her?'

'No. But I did see that boy, Ziggy. He dropped out of a tree just like last time.'

'What did you say to him?'

'That he really should think about varying those dramatic entrances.'

I folded my arms and put my head to one side. That just made Aiden grin even more.

'I asked if Xena was around. He told me to go away, though those weren't his *exact* words. I politely declined. He tried to make me. I stopped him.' Aiden examined the scrapes on his knuckles. 'When all of that was done, I asked him to pass on a message to Xena. That message being that I wanted to talk to her and would appreciate it if she turned up tomorrow at approximately four in the afternoon.'

'And what did Ziggy say?'

'He didn't say anything. He spat out a tooth and left.'

The sound of the afternoon song called us to class and we both turned towards the building.

'She won't turn up, you know,' I said.

'Oh, I think she will,' said Aiden.

'Why should she? Because you reckon she's got the hots for you?'

Aiden laughed.

'Well, probably. She's only human. But no, Ash. She'll turn up because I said I'd pay her to. In solid gold, actually.'

That stopped me in my tracks.

'You don't have any gold, Aiden,' I pointed out.

He turned to face me. 'True,' he said. 'But Mum and Dad do. Loads of it, in jewellery boxes all over the house.'

'And what? You think they'll just give some to you?'

'Nah,' he said. 'Unlikely. So I'm going to have to steal it.'

I spent the rest of the school day in a mental fog, so much so that Mr Meredith got quite stern with me, which was a first. But I couldn't get my brother's words out of my head. He was going to steal from Mum and Dad? That had to be a joke, right? This wasn't like Aiden at all. A thief? Someone who gets into fights (and for the first time not to protect me)? Mr Meredith asked him how he got the cut over his eye and Aiden said he'd slipped in the playground. He said it without hesitation and with complete sincerity. I was tempted to believe him and I *knew* it wasn't true. Could all of this be put down to puberty? I wasn't going to ask Charlotte and risk another lecture, but I supposed it was possible.

Nonetheless, it made me scared. Not just because I wasn't sure I liked what Aiden was turning into; I was worried I'd be undergoing that change myself. Maybe it had already started.

I didn't want to become a liar and a thief. I was pretty sure I'd be rubbish at fighting.

Dad sent the car for us, so I was able to grill Aiden some more on the way home. I decided not to talk about stealing – I'd convinced myself that he was joking about that, trying to wind me up. But one thing he'd said had stuck with me.

'Why four o'clock, Aiden?'

'Huh?'

'You said four o'clock for your meeting with Xena. That's after school. How could that work?'

'Oh, yes. Well, it's pretty simple, Ash. Five or ten minutes isn't going to be enough from my point of view and that's all the time I'd get if I did it like today, skipping out just for lunchtime. Four o'clock will give time for a decent conversation.'

'But we'll be going home from school then.'

'*You'll* be going home. I've got a meeting of the newly formed fencing club at school. You know, the kind of extra-curricular activity that our school is so famous for.'

'But there isn't a fencing club, Aiden.'

He laughed and put an arm round my shoulders.

'Ah. *You* know that and *I* know that, Ashleigh. But Dad doesn't know that, does he?'

'He'll find out.'

'Maybe. But not from me and not from you. And, anyway, so what if he does? What's he going to do to me, hey? No using my tablet for a week?' He gave a mock shiver. 'Oooh, I'm scared.'

I didn't say anything else on the drive home. I was too scared to talk to my brother in case he told me other things I didn't want to hear.

Dad swallowed the fencing club story at once. He even praised Aiden for his initiative in starting it (my brother added that little extra detail) and said he'd send the car at five o'clock. Dad also wanted to know whether I would be coming home at the normal time.

'I think I'll stay and check everything out,' I replied. I was careful not to mention the non-existent club because what I'd said wasn't strictly speaking a lie. I *did* want to check everything out. I didn't feel much better about myself, though. I couldn't ignore the fact that words can tell a literal truth, but still deceive.

'All good,' said Dad. 'And we'll maybe think about getting you all the right equipment if this is something you're really keen on. Just let us know.'

'Thanks, Dad,' said Aiden. 'That's very good of you. As always, generous to a fault.'

Dad gave my brother another strange look when he said that.

Later, in the pool, Aiden dived beneath me and tried to pull my legs down and give me a dunking, but I wasn't in the mood. So he bobbed at the edge next to me.

'So you're coming along to see Xena, Ash,' he said.

'Coming along to look after *you*,' I replied. 'The way you're behaving, you really *need* a minder, Aiden.'

He laughed. 'I feel safer already.'

'You were joking about stealing stuff from Mum and Dad, weren't you?'

'Already done it.' Aiden brushed his wet hair straight back over his head. 'A ring Mum has never worn, as far as I know, and a solid gold wristwatch of Dad's that's also not needed. I've stashed them under my bed. You can have a look at them later, if you want.'

'You can't just *take* those things.'

'Well, I did, sis. It was really easy.'

'It's wrong.'

'Why? Dad's got a whole collection of watches and he never wears any of them.'

'Nobody wears watches, because they're antiques,' I said. 'As you know. Dad's a collector.'

Aiden snorted.

'He's a collector? Okay. Right. He collects valuable things to stick in a drawer where no one will see them, not even him. They have no use whatsoever, they cost a fortune and they're not even decorative. At least the paintings Mum collects can be hung on the wall and admired. Their useless rings and watches won't even be missed, yet if you sold them they could probably feed a family for years.'

'Aiden, it doesn't matter what you say. Stealing is a crime and it's wrong.'

He hauled himself from the water and sat on the edge, reached back and grabbed a towel.

'We have more than we know what to do with. Other people are poor and starving to death. No one is hurt by this. For Mum and Dad it's a drop in the ocean. Probably less than that. For Xena it might mean the difference between life and death. How can that be "wrong", Ash?' He made the quotation marks in the air. 'Explain it to me. Show me exactly how I've sinned.'

And maybe I would have tried, but I knew that he would run rings around me with words that *sounded* fair and right and just, but which were really just bright make-up, covering up the ugliness beneath. I couldn't do it.

'Cheer up, sis,' said Aiden. 'It's not the end of the world. Hey, fancy a race? Two laps, freestyle?' He jumped back in.

I didn't fancy a race. I wanted to go to my room and cry. But I raced him anyway.

He beat me by three-quarters of a length.

11

Albert Street was just as deserted as last time but, if anything, I was more scared now. I remembered Ziggy suggesting a ransom. Maybe Xena had changed her mind and we'd be walking straight into trouble. It'd be our own stupid fault. What had she said last time? *Stay in your own world, you wouldn't like the real one.*

We should've taken her advice. Now we were alone and vulnerable, in dangerous territory, with a small fortune in the pockets of Aiden's trousers. I should have gone home at the normal time, left Aiden to it. If he wanted to put himself at risk, then that was his choice. No reason for me to do the same.

But he hadn't thought that when he dived into the river to save my life. He was there for me. Now I had to be there for him. I didn't really have a choice. But that didn't mean I was enjoying it.

'Let me do the talking, Ash,' said Aiden.

'Good luck with that,' I replied. If my brother could dismiss me with that phrase, I saw no reason not to use it myself. 'Hate to break it to you, bro, but the days of men being absolutely in charge are over.'

He glanced at me.

'Hate to break it to you, sis, but everyone's agreed with that sentiment for generations. Trouble is, nothing's changed.' He turned a full circle, checking we weren't being followed. 'And things definitely need to change. So, yes. You're right. Talk whenever you want.'

'Wow. I'm so grateful you've given me permission.'

He laughed. Funnily enough, I didn't feel like laughing. I was too busy checking out my surroundings and jumping at every imagined threat.

'Right again, Ash,' he said. 'Sorry. I'm being sexist. Forgive me and keep on pointing it out to me. Men either forget all the time, or don't care. I'm the forgetting kind.'

I wanted to continue the conversation. I wanted to point out that saying it's a woman's responsibility to remind men how to behave properly was sexist in itself. And this was the closest we'd come to a proper talk in... I couldn't remember how long. But the strange entrance to Victoria Park loomed before us and there was a tension in the air that made my words dry up. I checked inside the arch just in case there was a girl waiting, but it was deserted. The whole park seemed deserted. Aiden and I walked in about twenty metres and looked up into the branches of the nearest trees. Nothing there either.

'She won't come,' I said.

'She will,' said Aiden. 'I mean, I'm not trying to silence your views, but…'

'Oh, shut up,' I said.

'Bit harsh.'

We waited for ten minutes and I was on the point of saying we should go back when Aiden nudged me. At the far end of the park, a group of kids came through a gap in the trees and headed straight towards us. They fanned out as they reached the open, eight or nine in a row, a small girl in the centre.

'Don't they know how stupid that looks?' Aiden whispered to me, without turning his head. 'Are we in some kind of retro Western? If I had stagecoaches I'd get them into a circle.'

I didn't say anything. My brother might be able to joke, but my mouth was dry and I felt that familiar urge to visit the toilet.

'You do the talking,' I said, and Aiden laughed.

The group stopped about four metres from us. Xena took an extra stride forward, then paced a few steps from side to side, her brilliant green eyes never leaving Aiden's face.

'I thought I told you not to come back here,' she said. 'What's your problem, rich kids? All that money made you deaf?'

We didn't say anything. Out of the corner of my eye, I saw my brother clasp his hands in front of him and move his legs apart. The movement made a couple of the kids tense. We waited.

'Well?' said Xena. 'Nothing to say?'

'Sorry,' said Aiden. 'All my money has made me deaf. You'll have to speak up.'

It might have been my imagination but I thought I saw the flicker of a smile cross the girl's lips.

'What do you want?' she said.

'Just to talk,' said Aiden. 'And I'm prepared to pay you for your time.'

'Ziggy said. So show me.'

Aiden reached into his pocket and took out the ring and the watch. He held them out in the palm of his hand.

'One-carat diamond in the ring, I think. The wristwatch is a Rolex. Solid gold.'

'What's a wristwatch?'

'It's how people used to tell the time, back in the day,' I said. I don't know where I found the courage to speak, but the words were out there now. Xena turned in my direction. I was pleased. Up to this point she'd ignored me, as if I wasn't worth bothering with. 'You wouldn't believe how much this thing is worth,' I added.

'I probably wouldn't,' she said. 'I tend not to believe too much that strangers tell me.'

'My father paid one hundred thousand dollars for this watch,' said Aiden. 'That's worth a few minutes of your time, isn't it?'

Xena crossed her arms.

'I don't believe too much that strangers tell me,' she repeated. 'You really do have hearing problems, don't you?'

'Hey, look. Up to you,' said Aiden. 'If you can afford to give up one hundred thousand dollars because you don't want to talk, then okay. We'll just go.'

Xena laughed.

'I don't think so,' she said. 'There are nine of us and two of you. Ziggy told me you know how to fight, but your sister here…well, no offence, princess, but you don't scare me too much. So what if I decide to just kick your butts, take what you've got and—'

'Oh, shut up,' I said. I nearly yelled it. What the hell was I doing? All heads turned in my direction. 'This is stupid. My brother is trying to give you a small fortune and you don't even want to talk? What is wrong with you people? What is wrong with you?'

There was silence.

'How could I trade that thing, that wristwatch?' said Xena after a while.

'My dad would buy it,' said Aiden. 'I'll give you his details. Offer to sell it to him for eighty thousand and he'll think it's a bargain.'

'You stole it from him?' said Xena.

'Yes.'

'And you reckon he'd buy back his own stolen property?'

'In a heartbeat. He probably wouldn't even realise it was his.'

'I hate to say this,' said Xena, 'but I like you, kid. You have…*style*. Okay. You have twenty minutes. Not just for that stuff…' She nodded towards Aiden's hand, '…but because I like you. So. Shoot.'

'I want to talk to you in private.' He glanced over at me. 'Just the two of us.'

'Sure.'

'Wait a moment,' I said. I grabbed Aiden's arm and turned him towards me. 'What's this?' I whispered. 'All that feminist, hey you're right, I'm being horrible garbage and then you're cutting me out?'

'Can we talk about this later?'

'No.'

Aiden put both his hands on my face, cupped my cheeks.

'Please, Ash?' he said. 'Trust me on this. I have to do this one thing by myself. It's not because I don't trust you or I think you're inferior to me or…' He twisted his mouth. 'Anything,' he finished. 'But I'm…protecting you. I've always protected you, right? Let me do that one more time.'

I brought up my arms between his and swept his hands away from my face.

'You saved my life, Aiden,' I said. 'So let's be honest here. I owe you a favour.'

'And this is how I want you to repay it.'

'…But I hate this, you hear? I hate it.'

I walked straight up to Xena. She looked at me with what I thought was a certain amount of amusement.

'Here's what *I* want to ask,' I said. 'Why did you let us go? That last time. You could've held us to ransom, but you didn't, and I don't think that's because you're a kind-hearted person. No offence. So why?'

She looked up at me with those amazing eyes and it's probably my imagination but it was like she was seeing me properly for the very first time. And I could detect a battle going on in that face. Why should she tell me? It was none of my business, after all.

'Well,' she said finally. 'Looky here. The princess has a mind of her own. Okay. Why not? Here's the story. I had a twin brother once, princess. Older than me by four minutes, I was told. He died when I was a year and a half. Coughed up blood until there wasn't any left. Just a disease, they said. But I knew better. It was poverty that killed him.' She laughed and those white teeth startled me once more. 'I saw the two of you and … well, maybe I *am* a softie. But the pair of you reminded me of him. So I let you go. For him.' She tapped me on the cheek. 'I can't promise I'll make that decision again, princess.'

And we locked eyes for what seemed like minutes, but was probably only a few seconds.

'Thank you,' I said. 'And I'm sorry about your brother.'

But the moment was over before it had even really begun. Aiden and Xena stepped away and wandered further into the park, leaving me and the rest of the kids in an unfair showdown close to the park's entrance. Eight of them glaring at me. One of me, pretending I wasn't scared.

It was a long twenty minutes.

Finally, they broke apart and Aiden walked back towards me. Xena whistled and the rest of her gang walked towards her. The meeting was done and we headed off in opposite directions. I wasn't happy. I didn't know if Aiden was. His expression gave nothing away and he didn't say much on the walk back to school.

We leaned back into the soft upholstery of the car.

'Well?' I said.

'I've changed,' said Aiden. 'Since the accident, I've changed and I know you've noticed and I know you're worried.'

I was talking about his conversation with Xena and my brother knew that. But this was just as interesting and maybe more important. I also suspected the two things were connected.

'You're almost a different person,' I said. 'And yes, I'm worried. Of course I'm worried.'

'You know that old expression, "you need to have some sense knocked into you"?'

I nodded, but I don't think he noticed.

'In some ways, that's what the accident did. Before, Ash, it was like my sole purpose in life, my *only* purpose, you know, was to look after you, to protect you against all danger, every threat.' He sighed. 'Do you remember that lesson Mum gave us so many years ago? The duty of siblings is to catch each other if one should fall. This'll sound crazy, but I think I let that be the sole reason for my existence. Looking after you, making sure nothing bad happened. I never really thought about me and what I wanted.'

I thought about that and it was strange, but I felt like crying. I felt like crying because it was so obviously true. My brother never really had an opportunity to be himself and I'd just been a limiting factor on his development, stunting his growth.

'I kinda liked you protecting me,' I said. 'I felt safe.' My voice didn't break and I was grateful.

'I will still protect you, Ash,' he replied. He reached over and took my hand. 'That hasn't changed and it never will. But I'm beginning to think there are other ways to protect people. Maybe even that protecting people isn't the best form of protection. Do you know what I mean?'

I laughed.

'No,' I said. 'Because that doesn't make sense.'

But Aiden didn't laugh.

'We're like one of those fairy stories Mum used to read to us at bedtime, Ashleigh. A princess and her prince brother in our beautiful tower. Wonderful, glorious. Heroes. But we know nothing about the world out there, the farmers, the blacksmiths, the soldiers, the beggars, the drunks, the dead and the dying in their ditches, the filth and the squalor. The real world. We *need* to know about those things, Ash. We can't drift through life in privileged ignorance. We should help where we can. That's what makes us human. Or it should be.'

I thought about Charlotte and the brief glimpse I'd been given into her life and her way of thinking.

Her comments about Aiden and me, the implication that because we were rich, we couldn't understand the problems most people faced on a daily basis.

'That's what you talked to Xena about?'

'She taught me more in those twenty minutes than Mr Meredith could teach in ten years at school.'

'And what did you learn?'

'A bit about the dead and the dying.'

I was going to ask him to be more specific, but I knew he wouldn't open up. Maybe when he was ready, he'd tell me what he and Xena talked about specifically, but this wasn't the time or place.

'Do you think you're going through puberty, Aiden?' I asked.

He laughed and I was pleased; I'd asked the question partly to relieve the gloomy atmosphere left by his words. *The dead and the dying?*

'Probably,' he said. 'It's that time, isn't it? Hormones raging through your body, the mood swings.' He threw up his hands in mock despair. 'Oh, my God, the hair and the pimples!' He made his voice go all deep. 'Not the hair and the pimples, sweet Lord.'

I laughed with him. And for a while I could almost persuade myself that things were fine.

'You've changed too, you know,' he said as the car drew up to our front gates, which slid open.

'No, I haven't.'

But he carried on over me.

'You used to care about one thing only: Ashleigh

Delatour. Favourite subject. *Only* subject. The centre of the universe with everything revolving around you.'

The car doors slid open noiselessly, but we stayed where we were.

'Hey, Aiden,' I said. 'Tell me like it is. Don't spare my feelings.'

'That's what I was talking about before, Ash. I'm done with sparing your feelings, because although that seems like protecting you, it really isn't. Not many people liked you because you weren't interested in them. Do you remember that old gag? *But enough talking about me. Let's talk about you. What do you think about me?* It was made for you.'

I knew Aiden was right, but I was close to tears anyway. Again. I sat in the car, head bowed. Deep down, I felt I deserved this.

'The old Ash would have spat the dummy hearing this,' said Aiden. 'Tantrums. Tears. Throwing the toys out of the pram. But you've changed. You came with me to see Xena because *you* wanted to protect *me*. Dad told me about the gift they sent to that camp assistant's son on our behalf. You've cared for me while I've been ill. You even let me have Z stay in my room, when I know you were desperate to have him in yours. Hate to break it to you, sis, but you're becoming ... kind.'

'Now you *are* being horrible,' I said and we both laughed. 'Maybe that accident knocked some sense into both of us.'

'Or maybe we're both going through puberty.'

'Not the hair and the pimples!' I yelled.

We got out of the car. The doors closed behind us and the car drove itself off to the garage. Aiden took my hand once more and nodded towards the front door of our house.

'Ready for Disneyland, Ash? *The Happiest Place on Earth*?'

'What the hell is Disneyland, Aiden?'

'Never mind, Minnie Mouse,' he said. 'Ancient history.'

Mum was back from India and was bustling around the kitchen, preparing a vegetable curry. She hugged us both and then went back to chopping onions and grinding spices in a mortar and pestle.

'India is *the* place to go for vegetarian food, Ashleigh,' said Mum. 'Mind you, they've been specialising in it for thousands of years, but…my God, delicious. I brought back all these spices with me. Things you can't get over here. Cumin, fenugreek, coriander seeds, black cardamom, garam masala. You're going to love this.'

'Good conference?' asked Aiden.

Mum threw the spices into a frying pan and added a touch of vegetable oil. Almost immediately, the most amazing smell filled the kitchen.

'Very productive, thank you.'

'Did you find the poverty confronting?'

I glanced at Aiden. It seemed like a strange question. Well, not so much a *strange* question, but one that seemed…I don't know. Inappropriate. Mum obviously thought so too, because she stopped stirring for a moment and looked at her son.

'I didn't see any poverty, Aiden,' she said finally. 'I stayed in a very good hotel. But the whole reason I was there was *because* of poverty and starvation and how my company can help.' She went back to stirring, head over the pan. 'As you may or may not know,' she continued, 'India suffered more than most as a result of climate change and the resulting destruction of arable land. Many millions of people starved to death. My company is producing thousands of worker bots that will tend land and grow crops in places that people can't. We're feeding that nation, Aiden.'

'Made good profits on those bots, did you?'

This time, I couldn't help myself. I gasped. Mum threw down the wooden spoon into the frying onions and spice mixture, put her hands on her hips. The expression on her face was thunderous and I took a step back. Aiden didn't.

'The Indian government bought about half. We donated the others.' Mum was speaking slowly and clearly, as if trying to keep her words under control. I couldn't remember seeing her this angry. 'Why didn't we give them *all* away, Aiden? Is that what you're asking? Because we need money to continue our research into ways of helping people. Without funds going into AI, the world will slowly but surely die. *That's* what my company is doing.'

'Wow,' said Aiden. 'Saving the world. Impressive.'

They stood there for the best part of a minute, mother and son facing each other in a stand-off I didn't understand. In the end, it was Mum who blinked first. She picked up the spoon and continued stirring.

'Have a shower, prepare for dinner,' she said. 'It'll be ready in half an hour. I don't want to see either of you until then.'

Z was overjoyed to see Aiden. He whined, he whimpered, he jumped up my brother's legs, he rolled on his back on the floor.

'Boy, you've been doing a lot of training,' I said. 'Getting emotionally needy, Aiden, or what?'

Aiden knelt down and rubbed Z's belly. The dog squirmed in obvious ecstasy and almost twisted himself in two trying to lick Aiden's hand.

'He doesn't worship me like that,' I added.

'Because you haven't put in the training,' Aiden replied.

'Because he will only sleep in your room,' I said.

'Because you haven't put in the training.'

I sighed. I loved our dog, but maybe I'd just have to live with the fact that he preferred my brother's company. All the reading I'd done on cats and dogs had told me it was common for pets to prefer one owner over another. And I didn't want him to become a ... a ... I smiled. A bone that Aiden and I would fight over. That was the phrase.

'What else can he do?' I asked.

Aiden stood and clicked his fingers. Z jumped to his feet and sat at Aiden's, tail wagging, looking up in adoration. At another hand command he went around Aiden's legs and sat to his left, facing me.

'Impressive,' I said.

Aiden smiled. 'Oh, there's more. Ready, sis?'

'Sure.'

My brother pointed at me. 'Go,' he said.

Zorro didn't hesitate. He darted at me and sank his teeth into the calf of my right leg. It was so unexpected, I didn't even feel the pain for a second or two. Then I yelled.

'Leave,' shouted Aiden and the dog let go, sat down, tail wagging and looking up at me as if expecting praise.

'What the hell, Aiden?' I shouted. I bent over and examined my leg. A small dribble of blood oozed from a couple of puncture marks.

'God, sorry, Ash,' said Aiden. He came over and knelt before me. 'I didn't mean for him to do that. He's supposed to grab, but not with enough force to break the skin. I'm so sorry. Here, come on. Let's get some antiseptic on that.'

It took me a few minutes to calm down. The wound wasn't bad at all, little more than a scratch really, but it was the surprise more than anything that got to me. Aiden bathed the punctures and stuck on a band-aid.

'Guess I need to rethink that bit of training,' he said.

'Guard dog's good,' I replied. 'But not if he's going to bite all of *us*. That's not really the idea.'

'Let's keep this to ourselves, hey, Ash? I don't want any more confrontation with Mum.'

I agreed, but couldn't help but think confrontation was *exactly* what my brother seemed to be aiming for.

'Aiden. You'll be going into the clinic again tomorrow,' said Dad over our vegetable curry. Mum was right. It was delicious and creamy and tasted of … well, I didn't know vegetables could taste that good. I hoped she hadn't used up all those spices in the one dish.

Aiden sat at the table with us. I felt sorry for him. That green stuff for every meal. Not even a chance of trying a curry. That was bad enough, but watching us eat it must be torture.

'I thought I was done,' said Aiden.

'We thought so too,' said Dad. 'But your doctor rang up before you got back from school. Some blood samples they took were ruined at the lab, so they have to do it all again. Just a day stay, that's all.'

Mum was eating her curry very slowly and deliberately. She also was staying out of this conversation, maybe because she knew she and Aiden were likely to get into a fight if she said too much.

'Will this be the last time?' said Aiden. 'I can't tell you how tired I'm getting of being in that place.'

'Hopefully.' Dad took another forkful of curry. 'But it's the doctors who decide, not us.'

12

It wasn't a day stay, at all. Aiden was in for three days. When I asked Mum and Dad why, they said that there had been some complications in his treatment. Nothing to worry about, but the surgeons had gone back into his head to stop a little bit of bleeding that the tests had detected. All very routine, and he'd be coming home tomorrow. I was glad. I missed him. Z missed him as well and, although he slept on my bed for those three nights, I knew he really wanted to be with Aiden.

I was shocked when he finally got home. The head bandage was back on, though thankfully not the frame, and my brother appeared exhausted and not really interested in anything. Zorro went completely nuts when he came through the door, and jumped up, barking and whimpering. Aiden smiled and put a hand down to be licked, but even the dog couldn't seem to lift his spirits. He went to bed and didn't come out until morning.

I wanted to go and talk to him, try to cheer him up, but I worried that I'd be stopping him from resting, so I didn't.

He was slightly better the next day, but some of that fight seemed to have gone out of him. He answered Mum and Dad politely when they talked to him and he was very concerned about me, asking how school had been and whether I'd been okay without him there looking after me. That was puzzling in itself. This docile brother was much more like the old Aiden, but still...

'Mum?' I said. She was reading a book in the library, while Dad was tending to the vegetable plot. It was early evening, so the temperature had dropped considerably and it was pretty comfortable being outdoors.

'Hmmm?'

'Has Aiden got brain damage?'

Mum put the book down then.

'What makes you say that, Ashleigh?'

'Because he's having all these mood swings. Before the accident, he was pretty calm, then after he was... I dunno, a bit crazy there. I was just wondering.'

Mum patted the chair next to her and I sat down. She chewed on her bottom lip for a few seconds and sighed.

'We've been worried about Aiden too, Ash,' she said. 'I won't lie to you. You're not the only one to have noticed the changes in his temperament. He's always been such a... predictable child. You could rely on him one hundred per cent. But now... well, he's rather difficult, to be honest. His behaviour is... unexpected.'

'Charlotte said it was probably puberty. Hormonal changes. That would account for it, wouldn't it?'

Mum raised her eyebrows. 'Oh, you've talked to Charlotte about this, have you? That tells me a lot about how worried you are. Yes, puberty would explain it, but so would the head trauma he suffered on camp. And his mood switches started immediately after that. So I think you're right to be concerned, Ash. I really do.'

'But he's going to be okay, isn't he?'

Mum smiled and patted my leg.

'I'm sure he is,' she said. 'You know that your father and I will spare no expense – and that clinic *is* expensive – to get Aiden back to the way he was.'

'Oh, I don't want him the way he *was*, Mum,' I said. 'He's much more interesting now. Before, he was ... well, you said it. Predictable. I've always loved Aiden, but now I like him as well. Do you know what I mean? I'm all good with unpredictable, I just don't want him to be *ill*.'

Zorro started being a very bad dog indeed and this helped with Aiden's recovery.

A couple of days after he came back from the clinic, we both went for a swim. As always, Z paced along the sides of the pool while we did laps. He'd stopped jumping in and now appeared to be a little scared of the water. According to Mum that's because he was learning. 'A baby will have no problems with water', she said. 'But later it will learn to associate it with danger. That's why it's good to teach a baby to swim before it becomes scared. Leave it too long and then you have to train it to overcome the fears it's developed in the meantime.' Z, it seems, was employing something Mum called 'deep learning' to have a healthy worry about drowning, even though it was physically impossible for him to drown.

Anyway, Aiden and I were chatting after a few laps and we noticed that Z had disappeared. Aiden tried whistling, but he didn't reappear. After a few minutes we forgot about him entirely. I was asking my brother about the clinic. It had never really interested me before, but now I realised that the whole place, and what happened there, was a complete mystery.

'So what are your doctors like?' I asked. 'And the nurses?'

'I never see very much when I go to the clinic, Ash,' he replied. 'I go in and my doctor, Mr Sinclair, talks to me for a while in his office. Then the nurse – always the same nurse, chatty, friendly Sue who insists I call her Sue – she gives me an injection as I'm lying on a stretcher and then … well, I wake up in a private room. Mr Sinclair does some tests and then I come home. Bit boring, really. I've never even seen the operating theatre.'

'That happens every time you go in to have your intestines … scrubbed, or whatever?'

'Every time.' Aiden kicked off from the side of the pool and floated on his back. 'With the head injury I got at camp, it's pretty much the same deal. Except

this time, when I wake up Mr Sinclair gives me these ...
well, I suppose you'd call them intelligence tests.
A whole bunch of strange questions. I suppose they're
checking to see if my brain's still working as it should.'
He swept his arms out, tipped upright and trod water.
'Everyone's worried about my brain,' he said. 'You,
Mum, Dad. I wish you wouldn't. I reckon it's working
better than ever.'

Later, he knocked on my bedroom door.

'Come and see this, Ash.'

I padded along behind him to his room. I was surprised
by how he'd made it his own in such a short space of time.
He had a projection of the solar system on his ceiling and
this amazing miniature railway track. It was only a circle
of a metre in diameter and just one train ran around it,
but it was cute as anything. He'd been given it by Daniel
at school, who'd had it as a kid, but said he didn't want it
anymore. *I think I'm developing Mum and Dad's passion
for antiques*, Aiden had told me.

But when I entered his room, it wasn't any of that that
took my breath away.

'Oh, my God, Aiden,' I said. 'How did this happen?'

Almost every bit of material in his room – the
bedclothes, a shirt that had been slung over a chair,
a small rug next to his bed – had been ripped to pieces.
It was a mess. And sitting in the centre of Aiden's bed,
surrounded by chaos, was Zorro, looking very pleased

with himself. His tail wagged as he looked to Aiden for approval. I was able to work out the answer to my own question pretty quickly.

'Mum is going to go mental,' said Aiden.

Actually, Mum didn't go mental. Not at first. She found it interesting and quizzed Aiden on the training techniques he'd employed. When he told her about the hand gestures he'd been using to give commands, she nodded.

'Ah, that probably explains it,' she said. 'You've taught it that a movement of the hand means that something is expected of it. But its problem is that it sees *all* hand movements as a command. You were both in the pool when it disappeared off to do this, right?' We nodded. 'Then I suspect that when you were swimming, the dog watched your hand movements in the water and thought it was supposed to obey whatever that command meant. I just don't know why it would interpret it as a signal to destroy.'

A light went on over my head, but apparently it had also gone on over Aiden's. He explained to Mum how he'd trained Z to grab an object by pointing a finger and the verbal command 'Go'. He also confessed to the dog biting me at this command.

'You hurt your sister, Aiden?' Suddenly, judging by her tone of voice, I thought she would go mental after all. 'I can't believe you'd be so irresponsible. What on earth were you thinking?'

'It was an accident, Mum,' I said. 'Zorro was supposed

to grab me, but I guess he didn't know his own strength. It wasn't Aiden's fault.'

'I'm not so sure about that,' Mum replied. 'Not so sure at all. Anyway, I believe that's the explanation for the ripping up in your bedroom. The dog thought you'd instructed it to do that. It was just being obedient.'

'I didn't say the "Go",' said Aiden. 'And Zorro is a *he*, not an *it*.'

'I'm pleased you find it so convincing,' said Mum. 'But the dog is a machine. Never forget that. Anyway, the algorithm responsible for its learning obviously decided that part of the command wasn't necessary. I told you, it learns for itself and, like any real dog, or person for that matter, sometimes its learning is faulty and mistakes are made. Having said all that…'

Mum cocked her head and looked at Z. He was still on Aiden's bed, but now he was lying, head resting on his front paws and looking up at us with those big brown eyes. It was breathtakingly adorable, more so *because* of the mess around him. *I'm sorry*, he seemed to be saying. *I don't know what I've done wrong, but I'm sorry*. I was with Aiden on this. Z might be a machine, but he was a real dog as far as we were concerned.

'What?' asked Aiden.

'I put a limiter in its behaviour algorithm,' Mum said, though it was more like she was talking to herself. 'It shouldn't be able to override that, no matter the training you give it and the learning it does. I must have made a mistake somewhere.'

She stood for a few more seconds and then clapped her hands together, which made Z blink in surprise. I think Aiden and I did as well.

'Okay. I'll keep an eye on it. Now. You kids. First of all, clean up this mess. You know where to find fresh bedding. When that's done, you can make a start on retraining the dog.' She pointed at Z. 'It's meant to be a toy. If it destroys anything else then it will have to go.'

We must've both made groans of horror because Mum held up her hand.

'This is non-negotiable. I will not have a machine that can cause you physical harm in the house.' She looked at me. 'Whether it's by accident or not. So be warned. And if you want to keep your dog then I suggest you make your retraining of it really good.'

I can't pretend her words weren't scary. We loved our dog, even if he had bitten me, even if he had been naughty. But we both knew by the expression on Mum's face that she wasn't bluffing. I vowed that we'd work hard on training to make sure Z didn't destroy anything else in the house. But if he took a playful bite out of either of us ... well, we'd put up with that.

And keep it secret.

It was the last week of school and I must admit I was glad. We'd only have two weeks off before we were back again, but I was looking forward to the time away. Mum had even said that there was a possibility she'd take us with her on her four-day conference trip to Perth, which was scheduled in that break. That was exciting because Mum had never taken us away with her before. She explained that it was dependent on a number of things, the main one being, of course, the weather in what was left of Western Australia. There had been three cyclones that season that had come perilously close to doing to Perth what one had done to Darwin forty years before – levelling the city to the ground. Nobody there had had the energy, money or labour resources to rebuild it. Mum said she'd flown over the Top End once and the sea and the bush had reclaimed the city completely.

So, the weather was a key factor. And Mum said that even if we went we'd have to stay in the hotel during the day. In the evening she'd be able to show us some of the sights, her workload permitting.

We kept our fingers crossed.

But events made all of that irrelevant.

It started so innocently. It was Thursday afternoon – one day to go – and Mr Meredith was giving us a quiz about Australian history. Most of the class were feeling dozy; it was very hot outside and the air conditioning was having difficulty coping. Maybe that had something to do with it. But Mr M had made us all stand up while he asked us a series of questions that had true or false answers. Things like, 'The Great Barrier Reef was officially declared dead in 2030. True or false?' If we thought it was true, then we linked our fingers together and put our hands on our heads. If we thought false, then we put our hands on our hips. Whoever got the question wrong would sit down and the winners would stay standing. Then we'd be asked another question until there was only one left – the winner, who Mr Meredith said would get a totally underwhelming prize. He said it was based on a very old game called 'Heads or Tails', but no one in the class really cared about that, or the quiz. I went out in the second round, which wasn't a problem. I could sit down and drift off somewhere in my own head.

It got to where there were only three left – Daniel, Charlotte (of course) and Aiden. I suspect Daniel got there by watching what Charlotte did – a pretty sound strategy and one that must have occurred to Mr M because with only three left he got them to stand facing away from each other.

Daniel lost in the next round, which left two. I should've told Aiden to sit down as well. Charlotte never makes mistakes.

'Wonderful,' said Mr Meredith. 'Are you excited at our finalists? Slugging it out for the main prize.'

No, we all thought. Well, *I* thought, and I imagine my thoughts weren't too different from those around the room.

'Here we go. Maybe the final question, we will see. True or false? The highest temperature ever recorded in Australia was 59.8 degrees Celsius in Oodnadatta in South Australia.'

Charlotte immediately put her hands on her head. Aiden waited a few seconds and then put his hands on his hips. We had a winner. My money was on Charlotte. Obviously.

'The answer is...' Mr M tried to keep the suspense going, but probably realised there was no suspense to start with, so he gave up. 'That is true, so Charlotte is the winner. Well done, Charlotte. You have won—'

'That's wrong,' said Aiden.

That stopped everyone. For a moment we were all frozen. Charlotte beaming at her triumph, Aiden still with his hands on his hips and the rest of us just blank.

'I assure you it's not,' said Mr Meredith. 'I looked all this up last night to make sure, Aiden. I'm sorry, but that's the correct answer.'

'The highest temperature ever recorded was 61.1 degrees in Birdsville, Queensland,' said Aiden. Our teacher just stared at him. Aiden held his hands up in surrender. 'Look, I'm not bothered,' he continued. 'That's fine that Charlotte's won. Seriously.' He looked in her direction and gave a thumbs up. 'But I think you'll find that the temperature you looked up was the last *official* highest recorded by the Bureau of Meteorology. Birdsville got sixty-one plus about ten years after that but BoM had stopped keeping records by then because it was all meaningless. Point is, Birdsville was unofficially the highest but that record's probably been broken since. I mean, who knows?'

'You're a sore loser, Delatour,' came a voice from the back. Justin, a beefy kid with attitude who barely pretended to be interested in lessons. According to Charlotte he was going to inherit the family business and was just counting off the days until then. Mr Meredith had had trouble with him before.

Aiden turned.

'Not a sore loser, Justin,' he said calmly. 'Just trying to get the facts straight.'

Mr Meredith, perhaps sensing that it would be a good idea to intervene, held up his hands for attention.

'It's a good point, Aiden,' he said. 'I should've said the highest *official* record. Should we do another tie-break question? Charlotte, would that be okay?'

'Not necessary,' said Aiden. 'I'm happy that Charlotte's won —'

'Well, you sure don't *sound* happy, Arseon.'

Aiden turned back to Justin once more.

'That's enough!' shouted Mr M, but things had gained a momentum by then that was always going to be difficult to stop.

'Arseon?' Aiden said. 'That's your wordplay on my name, is it, Justin? Impressive. And I know that no one else in this class could have come up with such a witty remark at such short notice.'

'You being sarcastic?'

'Enough!' yelled Mr Meredith again. Aiden smiled. It was his calmness that unsettled me.

'Justin,' he said. 'I'm delighted to see that you're not letting an education get in the way of your ignorance.'

'What?'

My brother turned to the class. 'Our classmate may look like an idiot and sound like an idiot,' he said. 'But don't let that fool you. He really *is* an idiot.'

That did it. The next thing, Justin had launched himself at my brother, who calmly side-stepped, punching him in the gut as he passed. And then all hell broke loose. Mr Meredith tried to come between them, other kids crowded to get a better look and I tried to squeeze through the scrum to help Aiden. When I finally got there, he was sitting on Justin's stomach, his knees pinning the boy's arms to the floor. His fist was raised to punch him in the face.

'Aiden!' I yelled, but I don't think he heard me. Mr Meredith was holding on to his upraised fist, trying to stop it from descending. I went to the other side of my brother as he lifted his left arm. If he couldn't punch with his good arm, then he was obviously going to use the other. I tried to do what Mr M was attempting. I held on to his arm, but I knew I wouldn't have the strength to stop him. As it turned out, Aiden just twisted his fist and lashed backwards, catching me in the mouth. I felt the sharp tang of blood on my tongue and I fell back onto the floor, dazed.

Aiden must have glanced behind him and seen what he'd done, because the next thing I saw was his face above mine.

'Oh, my God, Ash,' he said. 'I'm so sorry. I'm so sorry. I didn't know it was you. I'm...'

But he didn't get to finish and I didn't get the chance to warn him. Over his left shoulder I saw Justin getting to his knees. His face was flushed with rage. He moved his right shoulder back and I tried to say something, I tried to tell my brother but it all happened so fast and it all happened so slow, maybe because of the knock to my head and the dizziness that resulted, but I saw the fist coming down and then I heard the sound of knuckles against bone and my brother's eyes widened and then turned up into white and the last thing I knew was his dead weight on my body.

The school nurse examined my face and said I'd got a cut lip and that I'd probably have bruising for a few days, but other than that there was no real damage. Once Mum had satisfied herself that I was basically okay, she quizzed Mr Meredith on exactly what had gone down. She'd already sent Aiden to the clinic in the car for yet another check-up on his head. He had come to within a few minutes and said he was all good, but naturally Mum wasn't taking any chances and insisted he be given the all-clear by a qualified doctor, rather than a nurse. The school nurse had pursed her lips at that but said nothing. Aiden grumbled, but there was no reasoning with Mum and I couldn't blame her. As I said to Aiden, there was no point taking a risk with his health. There had to be a good chance he'd got concussion and it was better to be safe than sorry. He just nodded at that and went meekly.

I didn't hear everything that Mum said to my teacher because they were locked in the principal's study, but judging by the amount of time she spent talking compared to Mr M (the closed door kept most of the sound in – most, but not all), I reckoned she was unimpressed with the school's track record of keeping me and Aiden safe. Getting over the fence to go to the park, then the disaster at camp and now this. I was worried Mum might not be so supportive of Mr M this time. I got the impression she thought once might have been accidental, twice was getting careless but three times was downright negligent. Anyway, I sat on a chair in the corridor and listened to the rumble of their voices, trying to make out the words but really thinking about my brother.

I wished he'd stop getting himself in trouble. And look after his head. Was that too difficult? Apparently it was. I'd have a good talk to him about that when he got back from the clinic.

The car returned and Mum and I finally drove home. She'd told Mr Meredith that we wouldn't be in for the last day of school, all things considered. Mr M promised that Mum and Dad would get a copy of the incident report that he would compile and that, unfortunately, he couldn't see an alternative to Aiden being suspended for some days next term. Of course, similar punishment would apply to the other boy involved. But Mum didn't seem to care about any of that. I wondered if maybe we were destined for enrolment at a different school or even, God forbid, another round of homeschooling.

Mum made me go over the whole thing once more on the ride back. I stressed that Justin had provoked Aiden and that it was Justin who'd started the fight.

'But Aiden was going to finish it, by all accounts,' said Mum. 'He was trying to punch that boy in the face before you got involved. Is that a fair summary?'

'Yeah, but...'

'And he punched you, too.'

'He didn't *punch* me, Mum. His hand caught my mouth, that's all. He was so upset when that happened. And that gave the other boy the chance to hurt *him*. He got punched in the head because he was trying to protect me.'

'Hmmm.' Mum just pursed her lips. But she stopped the questions and just stared out of the window for the rest of the trip. I was glad. My mouth hurt and I think one tooth was a bit loose, but I wasn't going to complain. Anyway, it gave me time to worry about my brother.

I had to tell the whole story all over again to Dad when I got home. Mum left me at the front door and drove off to the clinic to check on Aiden. I asked her to send him my love and she promised she would.

I tried swimming a couple of laps, but I wasn't in the mood and anyway, it wasn't as much fun by myself. So I tried playing with Z, but *he* wasn't in the mood for *that*. He just stared at the front door as if willing Aiden to walk through it.

'Hey, mutt,' I said. 'What about me, huh? What about some loving for me?'

But apparently there wasn't enough to go around. I video-called Charlotte instead and she wanted to go over the whole fight again, so I pretended I had to go to dinner and got off the tablet as quickly as I could. Her hologram seemed disappointed when it puffed into nothingness.

Mum got home about dinnertime. Dad had made a vegetable lasagne, but none of us were very hungry, so we picked at the food and left most of it. Mum normally wouldn't let that happen, so I knew she was really worried. She'd told me and Dad that Aiden was being examined and that he'd be staying overnight at the clinic again.

'He's starting to spend more time there than here,' I pointed out. I was trying to lighten the mood, but Mum and Dad didn't say anything and just continued toying with their pasta. I asked if she'd sent Aiden my love and she said she had, but I think she must have forgotten because she didn't look me in the eyes when she said it.

I spent some time in the library before bed, but once again I couldn't seem to concentrate. I wanted to video-call Aiden but Mum said he was under general anaesthetic and anyway, I knew that I was to leave him alone when he was in there. The mood in the whole house was pretty foul. At one point I heard Mum and Dad arguing in the kitchen. Their voices were raised, but it sounded like they were trying *not* to raise them and failing. I heard Dad say something about being devastated and I wondered if they were finally having that talk about him going back to work and if Mum was putting her foot down.

None of my business, so I kept out of the way. I had an early shower and played a video game on my tablet, but I couldn't even get into that. I was on the point of giving up and going to sleep when I heard shouting down the corridor. To be honest, there was swearing as well. Then footsteps up to my door, which was flung open. Mum was standing there, Zorro in her arms, and she was not happy. In fact she was furious.

'Your damned pet just bit your father,' she said. She thrust him into my chest. 'Keep it locked in here with you, do you hear me? I've had just about enough today.' And she was gone, the door slammed.

I knew what she meant. I'd just about had enough today as well. I hugged Z to me. Now I had to worry about him. What had Mum said? One more incident and 'it would have to go'? *Over my dead body*, I thought. She couldn't do that to us. We hadn't had time to do the retraining yet. She couldn't be so heartless. Could she?

It was a question that rolled around in my head as I drifted off to sleep.

I don't know why I woke up in the early hours of the morning. I don't know why I decided to go to the fridge. Maybe all that toying around with dinner had made me starving and that's what had woken me. I guess it doesn't matter now.

I was padding down the corridor to the kitchen when I heard voices from the media room. Mum and Dad. Talking. Maybe arguing. I should have just walked past, got a snack and headed straight back to bed. But I couldn't resist. I knew that what they were talking about concerned me and I had to know what it was.

The door to the room was slightly ajar and I pushed it open a little further, stepping noiselessly into the room. No one would see me, since it's set up like an old-fashioned cinema, seats all pointing towards the screen, the entrance at the back. Mum and Dad were on the front row, so I sat on the floor in the back row. I could hear everything now.

'You do know that Ashleigh will be destroyed by this, don't you, Chrissie?'

'Of course I know. I'm not stupid, Gareth. But this can't go on. It can't. I cannot risk it.'

My blood ran cold. Mum was going to take Zorro away from us. That was so unfair. I bit my bottom lip to stop myself from crying out.

'And so what are you going to do? Just tell her straight out?'

'Maybe that would be best,' said Mum. 'But no. I'll just say he died in his sleep. Of course she'll be upset, but she's young. She'll get over it in time. She'll—'

'I will NOT get over it,' I yelled. Tears were running down my face and every part of me was shivering. Mum and Dad had jumped to their feet and were watching me. I wanted to be more grown up. I wanted to show them I could be mature about things, reason with them, persuade them my dog would be okay, we'd all be okay. But my foot was stamping the floor and I was howling. 'You will not kill my dog, Mum. You will NOT.'

And then Mum had my shoulders in her hands, but I didn't want to look her in the face. I heard Dad say, 'Chrissie?' and his voice was worried, but Mum's grip was firm and I couldn't help myself. My face lifted and I met her eyes.

'I'm not talking about your dog, Ashleigh,' she said.

'Chrissie!'

'I'm talking about Aiden.'

'What?' My voice choked on a laugh.

'Chrissie? Don't.' But Mum never took her eyes from mine.

'It's time you knew, Ashleigh. It's time you knew. Aiden is not your brother. He's not even human. Do you understand?'

I shook my head. I was numb and none of this made sense.

'I made him, Ashleigh. I made him in my lab to protect you. Aiden's a machine.'

13

Dad made me drink a glass of water. I didn't want it and most of it spilled out of my mouth and onto the floor. They sat me on one of the chairs at the front and Mum got a cold towel and wiped my face.

'I can't believe you just did that, Chrissie.' Dad's voice.

'Are you feeling okay, Ashleigh?' said Mum.

I shook my head. The pattern in the carpet was shifting, small spirals of red and green twisting and turning. I was close to passing out. That was okay. I didn't like where I was. I didn't understand anything.

'Chrissie, we need to talk,' said Dad.

'No, we don't,' Mum replied. 'Ashleigh and I need to talk. Ashleigh and I *will* talk. We're not leaving this room until we do. Do you hear me, Ashleigh?'

'This is crazy…' said Dad.

'Gareth, do us all a favour and get something strong to drink from the kitchen. Whisky on the rocks for me, a diluted brandy for Ashleigh.'

'She's a child. Alcohol is not …'

'I *know* she's a child and I know she's in shock. A small brandy won't hurt. Now stop arguing and just go and do it, Gareth.' Mum's voice. Angry. Hard.

I put my elbows on my knees, my head into my hands. Dimly aware that, somewhere behind me, a door closed. I wanted to vomit but there was nothing there. Out of the corner of my eye I saw Mum doing something on her tablet. There was a loud click and then she was speaking.

'Gareth, I have locked Ashleigh and myself in the media room. You cannot come in. Do not try to override the security program. It won't work because the system will only answer to me. My daughter and I are going to have a conversation and I am going to explain everything to her. It may take time. It *will* take time.'

'Chrissie…' Dad's voice. Worried. Hurt.

'I'm turning off our communication channels now. Wait for us.'

Silence.

Mum was pacing in front of the media screen. I could only see her legs moving one way and then the other. It was really strange. There was a buzzing in my head.

'Ashleigh, look at the screen.'

I lifted my head. It didn't really matter if I lifted my head or not. There was a map of Australia up on the screen, but it was a strange and distorted one, bigger than the proper map. I recognised it from lessons at school.

'This was Australia at the beginning of the twenty-first century, Ashleigh.' Mum was off to my right but I didn't look in her direction. I just stared at the screen. She must have pressed something on her tablet because the image changed to the real map, the familiar map, a bit like the old one but shrunk around many of the edges.

'Rising sea levels, caused by global warming that melted the icecaps, did this to Australia in a very short period of time. A crazy percentage of people, eighty-five per cent is the accepted estimate, lived within fifty kilometres of the coast. Twenty million Australians, most of whom, over time, became homeless. You know this from school, right?'

I didn't say anything. I was fixated on the map. I couldn't see where home was. Mum waited a few seconds and then carried on.

'Some tried to migrate to other countries, but nearly all were turned back. Many people died at sea in ferocious storms that swept most of the world.' She gave a strange and twisted laugh. 'Historians have often said that's ironic since successive Australian governments had banned migration *to* Australia by boat. Now *we* needed help, but found we had to reap what we had sown.'

I wondered what Aiden was doing. Was he awake? Mum had said they'd tell me he'd died in his sleep. Did that mean he already had, or was that something that was going to happen? I tried to figure it out, but I couldn't make sense of it. There was a banging on the door and Dad's voice, muffled, shouting something. I couldn't tell what it was. After a while, it stopped. Mum was still talking.

'...and naturally one of the consequences of all this was that international trade more or less stopped, many of our farms were destroyed and we didn't have enough to eat. That, added to natural disasters – tornadoes, cyclones, blistering heat, torrential rains, brought the population to just over seven million. We had created global warming. Now it killed us in the millions.'

'Aiden...' I said.

Mum crouched down in front of me.

'What did you say, sweetheart? What did you say?'

But I couldn't remember. After a while, she got up and continued pacing.

'Australia was hit very badly, but many other places had it worse. It was close to an extinction event for humanity, but we survived, Ashleigh. Bruised, battered, but we survived. Many animals did not, as you know. There was once a time when Australia had a fantastic and diverse range of flora and fauna. Plants and animals.' I knew what flora and fauna meant, but it didn't matter. 'Most died out, the mammals first, but then birds and insects. And that made the environment, already crushed, even worse.'

She stopped for a while. I thought about asking if I could use the bathroom, but then I remembered there was a bathroom in the media room. I wasn't getting out of here until she was ready. A *machine*? How could my brother be a *machine*?

'What food we needed, we had to grow. But there was virtually no fuel for the engines – we used to use fossil fuel back then, rather than renewables. That was a large part of the problem. That's why the world now is basically vegetarian. The animals we used to keep for food would eat a huge amount of food that *we* could eat. A criminal waste of resources. It was wrong to eat meat then. It's even worse now.'

I kept zoning out, but my head was starting to clear. I missed a lot of what Mum was saying, but then I knew most of it anyway. A part of me wondered why we were going over history. Then she told me.

'I'm putting things in context, Ashleigh. Context is vitally important. Do you understand?' I might have nodded. Maybe I did, because she continued almost immediately. 'Governments came and went but most could do nothing. Then, about fifty years ago, a law was passed that stopped any woman having more than one child. Some people ignored it, mainly the people who live off the grid out there, the people who forage for themselves outside government control and outside the law. But the point is, Ashleigh, it was a *good* law. When there's not enough food, you have to control the population. If you don't, the lack of food will do it for you. Too many people starve already without us making it worse.'

More silence. But I knew it was going to end.

'Have a child and you are sterilised. Permanently. If you happen to be having twins or triplets, okay. You keep them, obviously, but then you're sterilised.' Long pause. 'This brings me to Aiden.' She sat on the chair next to me and for a moment I thought she was going to put a hand on my knee. Her fingers hovered for a second and then disappeared from my sightline.

'One thing that did improve after the catastrophes of global warming was investment in science. Because it was science that offered hope for the future of humanity. Editing the genes of certain foodstuffs so they could survive, thrive even, in a radically changed climate. Eventually, world governments will look more closely at space investment, getting us off this planet to another world where we can start again. Cynics would say, to destroy our new home again. But that's the future. For the time being, it's all we can do to survive here. One of the things invested in was AI, my specialist area. Artificial intelligence can do so much. It can learn, adapt, change. It can work out how to become more efficient at whatever task it's given and efficiency is more important than it's ever been. It's no exaggeration to say that AI is the key to our survival. In the last fifty years it's evolved at a *phenomenal* rate, an unbelievable rate – it would, of course. That's what AI is designed to do.'

Mum crouched down in front of me again, lifted up my chin with one finger. I didn't have the energy to resist. I met her eyes.

'Thirteen years ago I had a beautiful baby girl and I called her Ashleigh. But I knew she would be an only child. She *had* to be an only child because immediately after your birth I was sterilised. And I held you in my arms and I looked at your sweet face and I knew that if, by some genetic accident, I'd had twins, you would have a brother to look out for you, to protect you. What would happen to Ashleigh if her parents died? You were going to be alone and growing up in a harsh and dangerous world. That's when I decided I would *make* you a brother. And he would learn to love you and protect you and die for you if necessary.'

Maybe because I had been so out of it for so long, Mum didn't see my slap coming. It stung my palm, made a loud crack and turned her face to the side. She stayed that way a moment and then slowly turned back to look at me.

'Aiden had to return to what we called his clinic at very regular intervals.' She carried on as if nothing had happened. 'In fact, it was my laboratory, and there I made adjustments, to his size obviously, so that he appeared to grow along with you, and to his appearance, so it matched yours. I also had to update his learning algorithms, to ensure he developed mentally as a normal child should. Everything I did in Aiden's creation had one purpose. To protect you. And he did, Ashleigh. He saved your life.'

My brain wasn't working very well, but a sudden insight came to me.

'Aiden,' I said. 'AI.'

Mum smiled and I wanted to hit her again. 'Yes. The name I chose for him was … appropriate, one might say.'

She stood and resumed her pacing. This time I got to my feet. I nearly stumbled, but I wasn't going to carry on being someone half-in and half-out of this conversation. I needed to think. I needed to understand. I needed to concentrate.

'After the head injury, I checked over all his functions and they appeared normal. I did some deep searches into the various algorithms I'd installed and they all seemed to be working fine. But he had changed. He was becoming different and I worried that he'd lost sight of the sole purpose of his existence. Your safety. I tried to strengthen that algorithm, but he overrode it. And that was impossible. Aiden had become something I couldn't control and he was obviously capable of violence.' She grabbed my shoulders and gave me a small shake, as if I'd done something wrong. 'If he hurt you, Ashleigh, if he did something that brought about your death, there could be no other child. I cannot take the risk, you must understand that. Aiden will have to be shut down. It's the only way to be sure that your protector doesn't become your destroyer.'

I studied Mum's face. Even now, I was hoping that she would suddenly confess that this was all some kind of tasteless joke, a fantasy she had created to amuse me. A fairy story like those she'd told us when we were small. But there was only the ugliness of truth in her eyes.

'Is he still alive?' I asked. My voice was surprisingly firm.

Mum tilted her head to one side.

'He's still functional, yes. Unconscious, but still ... *there*, if that's what you mean.'

'I have to see him.'

She shook her head. 'That's really not a good idea, Ash. You will find it very upsetting.'

'Does he know what he is?'

'No. And I don't want him to know. Why upset him?'

'You're going to kill him and you're worried about his feelings?' I was becoming stronger by the moment and a deep, rich rage was burning inside me.

'I can't kill him, Ashleigh. He's not alive.'

'I have to see him.'

Mum shook her head.

'If I don't see him I will never speak to you or Dad again. That is a solemn promise. Look me in the eyes and tell me you don't believe me.'

Mum gave a short laugh and then stopped, almost like she was reminding herself that it was not appropriate under the circumstances.

'You're young, Ashleigh. You'll recover from this in time, trust me. And this is not something I'm doing lightly. I've thought long and hard. Your dad and I are very fond of him too, you know. He's been part of this family for nearly as long as you've been alive.'

I took another deep breath. 'I will never speak to you again,' I repeated. 'As soon as possible, I will leave home and you'll never see me. I will not communicate with you. Ever. If I have a child of my own, you will not see your grandson or granddaughter. You will not know he or she exists. I will not come to your funeral. You will not come to mine because you will not know that I've died. This I swear.'

Mum did look in my eyes then and I think she saw something to frighten her. I hoped so, because I'd meant every word.

'Okay,' said Mum finally. 'It's not a good idea, Ashleigh, and it will only make you upset, but you can have one visit to say goodbye.'

'I'll tell you when that will happen,' I said. 'Now, open the door. I want to go to my room and I don't want to see either of you again tonight.'

And she did. Dad was waiting outside the door and he tried to hug me but I brushed past him and went straight to my room. I wasn't able to lock it; Mum had all the controls to house security, so I propped a chair up against the handle. Zorro wagged his tail as I lay down on the bed and I hugged him close.

Then I cried for the rest of the night. But I didn't make a sound. I wasn't going to give my parents the satisfaction.

14

Dad knocked on my door early in the morning.

'Ash?' I didn't say anything. 'Ash? Are you okay?' I thought this was possibly the dumbest question anyone could ask under the circumstances, but I couldn't be bothered to point it out. I was tired. Tired in a way that had nothing to do with lack of sleep. It was in my bones. 'Ash, I'll have to break the door down if you don't say anything. You know that, don't you, sweetheart?'

'Go away,' I said.

'Are you okay?'

'No. Go away.'

There was a long pause.

'You can't stay in there forever, Ashleigh. I've got breakfast here for you. And a drink. You must be thirsty. Please come out.'

I thought about it. He was right. I couldn't stay in here

forever, mainly because if I did, I wouldn't be able to see Aiden.

'I've made you chips.'

That would've broken my heart, if it wasn't already in pieces. He'd made me chips for breakfast. Well, let's all carry on as if nothing has happened, shall we? Because there's no tragedy big enough that some fried potatoes can't make it all go away. Poor Dad. For a brief moment I felt sorry for him.

'I'm opening the door,' I said. 'But just you, okay? Mum can't come in.'

'All good,' called Dad. 'Just me.'

I pulled the chair from underneath the doorhandle and opened the door a crack. Why should I trust his word? Maybe Mum was there, behind Dad, ready to barge her way in. But she wasn't. Just Dad, with a stupid grin and a loaded tray. He came in, and placed the tray on my bedside table while I put the chair back under the handle. Then he sat down on the bed and patted a space to his side.

'You're not sitting on my bed,' I said. 'I'm sitting there.'

Dad looked around my room but there was only one chair and it was acting as a lock. I pointed to the floor.

'You stand,' I continued, 'or you sit there. Your choice.'

He stood, swaying slightly as he put weight first on one foot and then the other. I picked up the glass of water. Food didn't interest me, but I was thirsty and I needed to be hydrated. Whatever was going to happen, I had to be thinking clearly. I drained the glass, refilled it from the jug.

'We couldn't take the chance of losing you, Ashleigh,' said Dad. 'And we would have if it hadn't been for your mother and what she…did. You would've died on that camp. You know that.'

I stroked Z's fur and he lay on his side, tongue lolling in apparent pleasure.

'It was Aiden who saved my life,' I said.

'Yes,' said Dad. He at least had the grace to keep his head lowered. 'But your mother…'

'I want to talk to her,' I said. 'Not now. This afternoon. At two o'clock I will come to the living room and I will be asking questions. Tell her I want honest answers. This evening I will go to see Aiden. Tell her to arrange that or whatever she needs to do to make it happen. Can you do that for me, Dad?'

He nodded.

'I'm so sorry, Ashleigh.' He took a step towards me, but then reconsidered and backed away. 'I wish you could see how sorry, how…*distraught* I am. I loved Aiden. He has been a son to me, but…' I crossed my legs and waited for him to finish. I wasn't going to make this easy. Hell no, I wasn't going to make it easy for someone who already referred to my brother in the past tense. 'Your mother thinks…no, she *knows*, that this is the right course of action. I mean, I…Yes, it's hard. No, I don't mean that. "Hard" is not the word. It's a disaster. It's a…'

'Dad.'

He stopped talking.

'Tell Mum, okay?'

He nodded and backed away to the door.

'Take the food with you,' I said, 'but leave the water.'

He scurried to the bedside table, picked up the tray and placed the water jug next to my lamp. I took the chair away, opened the door and stood to one side to let him out. He stopped in the doorway.

'We didn't want to lose you, Ash,' he said again.

'There's more than one way to lose someone, Dad,' I said as I shut the door on him.

Maybe I should've eaten something, even though the thought made me want to throw up. But I needed a clear mind and my blood sugar must have been disastrously low. I knew Dad would bring those chips back in a flash, but I didn't want anything from them. The water would have to do. Maybe hunger would sharpen my mind, rather than dull it. Because at two o'clock I would be a defence lawyer. Mum, the prosecutor, would be arguing for the death penalty and she's educated and super-intelligent and articulate and... and ruthless.

I had an oral presentation to prepare. I suck at them. Always have. That would have to change.

Mum sat on the couch in the living room. The windows had been dimmed, but there was still plenty of light. She didn't look good, as if she hadn't had any sleep either. I rummaged through my feelings to see if I could find any sympathy. Nope. I'd used it all up. Dad sat at her side. He was chewing his lip and one hand plucked at his earlobe. Mum was like a statue. I took the armchair opposite, a glass coffee table between us. That was another antique, like the couch and the chairs and the paintings on the walls. I used to think the whole place was beautiful. I didn't feel that way now.

'Aiden doesn't have to die,' I said. Mum held up her hand, but I knew what she was going to say. I'd had plenty of time to think all this through. 'You were going to say he has never been alive, in the biological sense, so he cannot die. That's just words. I'm going to talk about life and death. You might not like those terms, but to be honest, I don't care. We will not be arguing about the meanings of words, because that's just going to get in the way.'

Mum wanted to say something, she wanted to argue. I could see it in her face. But she nodded, folded her hands in her lap, fixed me with her eyes.

'Okay,' I said. 'So, I'll come back to that, but I want to ask a couple of questions first. Is that goo he eats vital to his survival?'

Mum shook her head. She was on solid ground here. We were talking about facts, rather than feelings, and Mum always was the master of facts.

'A cyborg, or whatever word you want to use – a humanoid AI doesn't require food. None of the machines I make would have any use for food. Look at your toy dog. Not that they would be given any regardless, since there's barely enough to feed people. As you know, that's the reason pets are illegal.' I could tell she wanted to stand and pace while giving a fascinating lecture on the subject, but I wasn't going to let that happen. I needed to keep *my* agenda in focus.

'So why the goo?'

'If I wanted him to pass as human, he had to eat *something*,' said Mum. 'Hence the goo, which wastes no foodstuffs.'

'Klinsmann's disease?'

'My invention.'

'It's on the internet. I've looked it up.'

'Of course it is. I made sure of it.'

I nodded.

'How does he function then? I eat food, which is converted to energy. Where does Aiden get his?'

'It's a good question.' I really wanted to tell Mum to go to hell. This wasn't a lecture theatre and I wasn't a student to be patted on the head for being a bit bright. But I had to keep my emotions in check. If I lost control of them, then I would lose everything. There'd be time for emotions later. 'In fact,' Mum continued, 'your brain requires less energy than used to be consumed in one of those old-fashioned bulbs in lamps. Nearly all your energy goes into metabolism and the human body is a shockingly inefficient system. Put simply, Aiden's body *is* efficient and he runs on renewables – the sun and the wind basically.'

'What actually happens when Aiden goes into that clinic if it's got nothing to do with cleaning his intestines?'

'I told you. Modifications to his appearance to give the illusion of growth, and checking out the artificial neural networks that enable his learning capabilities. Tweaking those if necessary. Just recently, when his behaviour changed after the skull trauma, I tried to alter the algorithms back to the original setting, remove any possibility of violence. I failed. I tried so hard, but I failed.'

'What would happen if Aiden never went back to the clinic?'

Mum frowned.

'Well, he wouldn't grow, obviously. He would stay the same, looking like a thirteen-year-old boy for ... well, forever, I suppose.'

'It's interesting,' I said. 'Whenever you talk about Aiden, you say "he". You might try to be the cold, hard scientist, but you see Aiden as a person. You see him as your son.'

There was a flash in Mum's eyes at those words, but it was difficult to read it. She steadied herself and it obviously took an effort of will.

'Would you prefer if I referred to the machine as "it", Ashleigh? Would you?' She took a deep breath. 'I thought not. And if you think that I'm enjoying any of this then you are wrong. *Wrong*. I feel, I feel ...'

'Spare me,' I said. 'So, Aiden doesn't have to die. You can just let him be.'

'I've explained this,' said Mum. 'He should not be behaving in the ways he's behaving. I put limiters on the AI neural networks that make it impossible for him to commit any acts of violence. Clearly he has found a way to get around them or remove them altogether. He was created to protect you, Ashleigh. Now he could hurt you. He might kill you.'

'Aiden would never hurt me.'

'He already has. You say by accident, but the point is, you just don't know. *I* don't know and I made him. He might have killed that boy in the classroom fight. He might kill you.'

'Okay.' I'd got to this point quicker than I'd planned, which probably showed how little headway I'd made against Mum. It was clear that me just saying Aiden would never hurt me wasn't going to cut any ice. 'In that case, leave him in the clinic. Keep Aiden locked up there, where he *can't* do any harm. I could talk to him all the time and visit regularly. It would be just like having a brother who was very ill and wasn't able to leave hospital. There's no need to kill him.'

Mum did stand now, but she didn't come anywhere near me, for which I was grateful. Instead, she moved to the window, unfolded her tablet from her pocket and punched in some command or other. The windows changed from opaque to clear. She stood with her back to me and looked out over our garden, the lines of vegetable plots stretching into the distance. For a moment, I seriously thought she was considering my idea.

'When I created Aiden, I did something illegal,' she said, her back still to me. 'The law is very specific on AI. All devices must be registered. I didn't do that with

Aiden. Or your dog, actually. The reason why they must be registered is so that if there are any...malfunctions, swift action can be taken. By swift action, I mean shutting down. Leaving Aiden in the clinic would serve no purpose and it would certainly put me in prison.'

'Maybe you deserve that,' I said.

Mum turned then. There was a small smile on her face.

'Maybe I do,' she said. 'If going to prison was the price to pay for protecting you, then I would consider it a bargain. But I told you. Leaving Aiden as he is would serve no purpose.'

'I don't understand.'

'Have you heard of Stephen Hawking?'

'He was a brilliant scientist, I think.'

Mum nodded. 'He was, indeed. One of the greatest minds of the last couple of hundred years. He was worried about the future of artificial intelligence. He predicted, and it's since come true, that advances in AI would bring about a revolution in machine thinking. Our human minds are slow. We evolve, but evolution takes a long, long time. Millions of years. What deep neural network AI learning does is reduce those millions of years of learning into weeks, days, hours...seconds, maybe. We just don't know. And imagine a machine that can build a better version of itself and then a better version again and so on, all without human interference. We think we are so much more advanced than an ant. An AI machine could make us seem like intellectual ants in comparison to its mind.'

'But a mind like that would solve all our problems.'

'A mind like that probably wouldn't *notice* our problems. When was the last time you worried about a problem an ant might be experiencing?'

'You're talking about evil machines. Aiden is not evil.'

'I'm not talking evil. I'm talking overwhelming *competence*. If humans get in the way of that competence, there's no telling what could happen. I suspect we'd be brushed aside. Like an ant.'

'Aiden is not a super-intelligent machine. He's just a boy.'

'He is now,' said Mum. 'But I come back to what I said before. He has worked out a way to get past the restrictions I put on him. He's out of control, Ashleigh. I have no idea what he could become, but I can guess it won't be anything like the kind boy you've always known. And that's why you should remember him that way. The brother who saved your life, rather than the advanced AI that destroyed humanity.'

'This is stupid.' I was panicking. I couldn't argue against all these things. Me against possibly the world's greatest expert on artificial intelligence? I'd hoped to find a crack in her logic but now I realised I hadn't had a clue in the first place.

'*I* was stupid,' said Mum. 'I was stupid to build him in the first place. I should've accepted that you would be an only child, like the vast majority of children brought into this world. But I wanted better for you. And I risked too much to make that happen. I was selfish. And now we're all suffering because of it. I'm sorry, Ashleigh. I'm so sorry.'

'But doesn't the fact that you don't know what kind of a genius he might become, mean you should continue to study him?' I'd found another proposition, a last-ditch one. It sounded good. It sounded like the kind of argument a scientist would like. 'You could learn so much from an AI like Aiden. All you'd need to do is work out a better … what did you call it? A better limiter on his mind.'

Mum sighed.

'Wouldn't that be good?' she breathed. She made the windows dark again. 'Someone once said about AI that people could stay in control because there's always an off switch. Pull the plug, problem solved. And there's another story. A person says to a super-intelligent AI, "Is there a God?" And the AI says, "There is now," and makes the plug disappear.'

'That's dumb,' I said. 'That's science-fiction, not science. Aiden couldn't destroy the world if he's locked in a room.'

'I could lock you in a room,' said Mum, 'and you'd have access to the internet via your tablet. You could open and close doors around this house. You could adjust the lighting and the heating. In short, you could make changes in the world. The kind of AI I'm talking about wouldn't *need* a tablet. It could control everything remotely from its mind.'

'It's fantasy,' I said.

'It's possible,' said Mum. 'Probable, even.' She sighed. 'This conversation is over, Ashleigh. I will take you to see Aiden tonight because I gave you my word. You will say goodbye and afterwards I will shut him down. I have no choice, but I am sorrier than you'll ever know.'

And with that all my arguments melted away, all my resolve to be logical, cool and reasonable. I sobbed. I lay on the floor, curled into the foetal position, and I sobbed. At some point I think I felt Dad's hand on my shoulder.

15

I stood under a cold shower for half an hour. Actually, it wasn't cold, it was freezing because I'd programmed it that way. Each pulse of water was like a needle of fire in my skin. I didn't think I could stand it, but then I found I could. You can get used to anything after a while. Maybe you can even get used to the inevitable.

Afterwards, I took considerable time working out what to wear. In the end I chose a yellow dress that Aiden had said he'd liked one time. Yellow's his favourite colour, so it was doubly appropriate. Black sandals. Then I put my hair up, keeping it in place with a yellow band. I looked at myself in the mirror. The overall effect was wrong. I looked like deformed sunshine, but I couldn't be bothered to change. And I so rarely wore dresses anyway. What was I trying to do? Make this out to be a time for celebration? I couldn't bring myself to care.

I folded the tablet and placed it into the side pocket of my dress. Then I picked up Z.

'We're going to see Aiden,' I said. His tail wagged at the name and that almost started me crying again. But it was important to stay in control. My brother deserved that. He deserved a lot more, but I could only give what I had to give. 'You behave yourself, okay?' I whispered into Z's ear. 'No biting ever again, do you hear?'

Mum and Dad were waiting for me in the kitchen. They both looked upset, but you'd have to be a monster not to be. Then again, I was still working through my feelings and my judgements. Maybe monsters could fake all that stuff.

'The car's ready,' said Dad. 'Are you?'

'No,' I replied. 'But I never will be. So let's just go and get this done. Zorro and I will travel in the back, alone.'

Mum simply nodded. We trailed out into the dark and the car drew up, doors opening. Dad got into the driver's seat and Mum sat next to him. Z and I climbed in the back. I always used to know how stressed Dad was feeling because he chose to drive, rather than letting the car have control. It was something to do with him using his hands, a nervous gesture. It didn't matter as long as no one tried to talk to me.

No one did. I kept the windows on clear, so I could see something of the scenery as we drove. As always, there were hardly any cars on the roads. Few people could afford them and there weren't that many places to go anyway.

I knew from history lessons that Sydney used to be a huge city with all these attractions. Theatres, restaurants. I'd seen pictures of the Opera House before it was destroyed by a tornado many years ago. Life seemed so much better then. Now, as I looked out over the deserted streets, the place appeared as bleak as my mood. In the distance the sky flickered with lightning and far off there was a low rumble that I could almost feel through the car's wheels.

I wondered how the majority of people lived in a world like this. If you didn't have solar sails or panels (poorer people used recycled panels from the old days, so I'd been told) then you'd have no electricity for lighting or cooking. In old Sydney there were loads of shops, selling all sorts of things. Massive places where you could buy whatever you wanted. Now, there weren't even food shops, let alone any other kind. In fact, the whole idea of shops seemed crazy to me. Why advertise you had anything of value? It was an invitation for thieves.

For some reason I thought about Xena. I still didn't know what she and Aiden had talked about, that last time in Victoria Park. I didn't think I was going to waste my time tonight asking Aiden about it.

It took about half an hour to reach the clinic. I knew we were approaching because I could see the lights before I saw the protective fencing and the guard huts. A couple of searchlights played across the landscape around the building. All hospitals have armed guards. There are drugs in there and, probably more importantly, food for the patients who can afford to be admitted.

This was a private research lab. Mum's property. And she would have it well protected.

We drew up to the gates and Mum pressed her finger against the electronic pad at the side. Whatever security system was being used, it recognised her fingerprint and the gates slid open. Dad drove through and parked close to the entrance. For a few moments, no one moved and then the car doors opened. I hugged Z close as I stepped out, lifted my face to the sky. There was going to be a storm. I could taste the electricity on my tongue. I could also taste guilt. I had talked to Mum about Aiden's behaviour. I had asked whether he had brain damage. I'd been very clear about his strange mannerisms. And, in doing all that, I'd provided her with more evidence that she could use against him. I'd been a key prosecution witness at my own brother's trial.

Would I ever be able to forgive myself?

I thought not.

Dad made a movement to take my arm, but then thought better of it. I climbed the steps to the laboratory ahead of my parents, concentrating fiercely to make sure I didn't stumble. I almost burst into tears when I got inside. It was all set up as if it really was a clinic. There were signs pointing to presumably non-existent haematology labs and x-ray departments and ear, nose and throat clinics. Aiden had come through these doors so many times and he'd believed the lies my mother had spun. He'd gone willingly for what he thought were medical procedures, trusting his mother. Who wouldn't trust his own mother? He thought he was a patient. In fact, he was a lab rat.

I stopped for a moment, hypnotised by the illusion, but Mum swept past me.

'This way,' she said, walking briskly down a corridor to our left. I followed, Dad bringing up the rear. We eventually arrived at a door at the end of the corridor. There were a couple of chairs up against the wall and a keypad set into the door.

'Aiden's in here,' said Mum, her hands reaching towards the pad.

'Wait,' I said.

I tried to control my breathing, because I was on the verge of hyperventilating. And now I felt dizzy. I sat in one of the chairs and tried to make my arms less tense. I realised I'd been holding Z too hard and he was looking at me in confusion. I scuffed him behind the ears and he relaxed a little.

'You stay out here,' I said to my parents. 'Me and Z go in alone.'

'Okay,' said Mum, 'but when—'

'When I come out again,' I continued, 'I will be upset.' Not for the first time, it struck me that some words in the English language are pathetic and weak and useless. I took another deep breath, but it didn't seem to help. 'I will be upset,' I repeated. 'No one is to say anything to me. I don't even want to see you. And I will not stay here while you … while you …' I bit my bottom lip and the quick pain helped me regain control. 'I'll go straight home. Program the car. Then … program it to pick you up afterwards. Or not, I don't give a damn. I will be in my bedroom, but you are not to come anywhere near me until *I* decide. Is that understood?'

'Ashleigh …' said Dad.

'Yes. Understood,' said Mum.

I stood, but had to put a hand against the wall when my knees threatened to buckle.

'Open the door,' I said.

Aiden lay in a hospital bed. He was reading a book and there were three or four pillows behind his back, keeping him propped up. Hearing the door open, he turned his head and did a double-take when he saw me.

'Ashleigh! What are you doing here?'

The dog twisted and squirmed in my arms and I had to put him on the floor. There was no choice; he was so excited to see Aiden that there was no holding him. As soon as his paws hit the ground, he scrambled across and jumped on the bed. Aiden laughed and put out his arms, but the dog launched into his face, licking frantically wherever he could find flesh. The dog's whole body was charged with joy. It took Aiden a good few moments to settle him down, by which time I'd sat on a chair by the side of the bed. Z had also given me just a few seconds to find my composure. Or the illusion of it.

'Hey, bro,' I said. I tried a smile, but it didn't feel right.

'What are you doing here? I thought you weren't allowed in.'

'I thought I wasn't, too,' I said. 'But I threw a hissy fit, said the dog was going crazy missing you and that we had to come in to visit.'

'And that worked?'

'No,' I said. 'So we weren't allowed. This is all an illusion.' I don't know where I was finding the words. They rolled off my tongue and I had no idea whether I was making any kind of sense or not. But Aiden smiled, so I guess they did. And his smile nearly broke my heart all over again.

'The dog missed me?' said Aiden, rubbing behind Z's ears. 'But my sister didn't? Is that what you're saying?'

'Of course I missed you. Like a hole in the head. Which is kind of ironic, when you think about it, since that's the reason why you're in here.'

'You've turned into a comedian.' He put on a spooky voice. 'What have you done to my sister? I want her back.'

We sat in silence for a few moments. I knew I couldn't keep this up for long. There was a cyclone of emotion breaking against the barriers I'd put up and I knew they couldn't hold for long. And when they were blown away, I'd be no match for those destructive forces. That wouldn't be fair to Aiden. Not at the end. At the end, I couldn't do that to him. Suddenly a monstrous crash of thunder made the room's windows rattle and a flash of lightning painted the walls silver.

All the storms were coming together.

'I have to go, Aiden,' I said.

He looked pained. 'You've only just arrived,' he said. 'Talk to me a bit longer, Ash. It gets lonely in here and I don't know when I'll be coming out.'

Another section of the defence crumbled.

'I have to go.' I stood and plucked the dog from Aiden's hands. Z didn't look happy and I had to hold him firmly to my chest. 'Did I ever tell you how much I love you, Aiden?'

'Now you're getting weird, Ash. What's going on?'

'You saved my life and I love you. I loved you when you didn't save my life.'

'Ash?'

But I had turned away. I opened the door, head bent, the dog clutched to my chest, the tears starting to flow. Maybe I was aware of my parents sitting on the chairs by the wall, standing as I rushed past. But I don't think so. I don't think I was aware of anything. Not the running down the corridor, out through the doors and into the blinding rain. I don't remember the car sliding up and a door opening. I cannot recall the journey home through the wind and the hail and the lightning flashes breaking the night. I have no recollection of closing my bedroom door, throwing myself on my bed and surrendering myself to despair.

16

I don't remember those things because they didn't happen. They are what I imagine my mother *thought* was happening. This is what did.

Aiden lay in a hospital bed. He was reading a book and there were three or four pillows behind his back, keeping him propped up. Hearing the door open, he turned his head and did a double-take when he saw me.

'Ashleigh! What are you doing here?'

The dog twisted and squirmed in my arms and I had to put him on the floor. There was no choice; he was so excited to see Aiden that there was no holding him. As soon as his paws hit the ground, he scrambled across and jumped on the bed. Aiden laughed and put out his arms, but the dog launched into his face, licking frantically wherever he could find flesh. The dog's whole body was charged with joy. It took Aiden a moment to settle him down, by which time I'd sat on a chair by the side of the bed.

'We don't have much time, Aiden,' I said. 'You must listen closely and do exactly what I say. Do you understand?'

He laughed. 'Not exactly the hug I was expecting under the circumstances, Ash—'

'Aiden, listen.' I took his hand in mine. 'Keep quiet and listen. You will die unless you do exactly what I say. This is not a joke. This is not an exaggeration. You *will* die.'

He shook his head.

'Remember the camp, Aiden,' I said. 'I didn't really know what was happening, but you saved me. Now *you* don't know what is happening and it's my turn to save you. Do you trust me, Aiden?'

'Yeah, of course, but…'

'We are going to swap clothes and I am going to get into that bed and pretend to be you. You will take the dog and you will open that door. Keep your head right down. Pretend to be upset, if you can, but whatever you do, don't stop. Mum and Dad are out there in the corridor. Do not speak to them, no matter what happens. Run as quickly as you can to the outside door. The car will be waiting for you. Get in. It will start to take you home.' Aiden's face was full of confusion and questions, but I ignored it. 'This next bit is very important. I don't know how long I will be able to pretend to be you, but sooner or later, they'll know you're gone. So as soon as possible, use the emergency override stop button in the car, get out and run. Do not go home. Find Xena. Your tablet is in the pocket of my dress. I will call you as soon as I can.'

'But this is crazy, Ashleigh. You can't expect me to do all this without any explanation.'

I was already pulling my dress off over my head. I threw the headband onto the bed and kicked off my sandals.

'You'll get an explanation. But now, I need you to get out of bed and change clothes with me.'

'You're serious.'

'Deadly. Now hurry up.'

'But…'

I wanted to shout, but that was impossible. So I grabbed him by the shoulders and shook him.

'Do it, Aiden,' I hissed. 'Do it now.'

And he did. I helped arrange his new clothes and I put the headband on him, sweeping the hair from his face. Then I stepped back and looked him up and down. Obviously, it helped that we are identical twins. What looked back at me was exactly what had looked back at me from the mirror at home. I knew that the way he walked would be different, but no one would be able to pick that up quickly, especially as he would be running. I tugged down on one side of the dress and nodded. Aiden's eyes were still confused, but there was fear in them also. I didn't know whether that was because he genuinely believed his life was in danger or whether he thought his sister had gone mad.

'I haven't gone loopy yet, Aiden,' I said, and hugged him close. 'That's just the rest of the world.' I pulled away but held on to his hand. 'Stay safe, brother. Promise me.'

'I promise,' he said.

'Your face is a promise,' I said and he laughed but it cracked a little.

I pulled back the bedclothes and got in. They smelled of Aiden. Z gave my hand a nuzzle and then looked from me to my brother and back again. If ever a dog was confused...

'Take Z,' I said. 'Then go quickly. Remember, head down, run and don't stop for anyone. Get to the park and wait for my call.'

Aiden took the dog, cradled him in his arms. I thought for a moment he was going to say something, maybe come over and give me a hug.

'Go *now*,' I said.

And Aiden turned, opened the door and was gone. As soon as he left I twisted onto my side, facing away from the door, and pulled the covers over me. I hadn't rescued Aiden yet. If Mum discovered the swap soon, she would reprogram the car to stop before it got out of the clinic's grounds. I had to buy Aiden time – at least five minutes, more if I could manage it. Every second counted. And that meant I mustn't say anything when my parents came into the room. It's possible they would think I was Aiden just by appearance – we *are* identical – but my voice would definitely give the game away.

Thirty seconds went past and then I heard the door close, footsteps approaching the bed. I couldn't pretend to be asleep. No one would believe that within seconds of my sibling leaving, I'd drop off. The only option I could think of was to fake being upset. So I made my shoulders heave a little, as if I was sobbing but trying to keep it under control.

'Aiden?' Mum's voice. I didn't respond. She put a hand on my shoulder, but I jerked away from it. If it seemed I was angry and upset with her, it would explain why I wasn't speaking. But I could only do this for so long. I checked my mental clock. Just under a minute. Aiden would probably be leaving the building about now, looking around for the car.

'Aiden. What's the matter?'

I brought my right arm out from under the bedclothes and waved it at her – a 'go away' gesture. I really wanted to turn to check if Dad was with her. Maybe my instructions had been ignored. Maybe Dad had followed his apparently distraught daughter to the car to offer comfort. That would mean disaster.

'What's the problem, son?' Dad's voice. I breathed a little easier. Just over a minute. He should be in the car by now. Another minute and he'd be through the gates. I didn't say anything, just drew the clothes tighter around me and moved towards the edge of the bed as if trying to get further away from their voices.

'Has Ashleigh been talking to you?'

I risked it this time. I turned and dipped the bedsheet to just below my nose. I guessed my eyes must be red, but I screwed them up anyway. I nodded and then turned away again.

'What has she told you? Aiden, what did she say?'

I made my sobbing louder and more violent. There was silence and then I heard Mum and Dad whispering. They'd obviously moved away from the bed and were discussing possibilities. That was good. I hoped they'd discuss them at length. A minute and a half. He'd still be in the grounds.

'Did she tell you what you are, Aiden? Is that why you're so upset?'

This time I howled. I figured howling or hysteria would be kind of gender neutral. We all look pretty much the same when we're emotionally out of control.

'Listen to me, Aiden.' Mum's voice, almost shouting. 'I need to explain some things to you.'

But I howled louder. My throat was hurting, but that didn't matter. Two minutes, maybe slightly under. I imagined Aiden in the back seat of the car, hugging Z to him, the gates sliding open as the car approached. A few metres, a few seconds from freedom.

Dad came round the other side of the bed. Now I had them on both sides, so I buried my face beneath the blanket. I could feel his hands on my shoulders and I squirmed. But he didn't loosen his grip.

'Aiden!' he shouted. 'Whatever your sister told you, it's not true, all right? It's not true. Everything's fine. It's all going to be okay.'

That almost took my breath away. Right there, right at the end, they were going to lie to him. Pretend everything was going to be wonderful. I think that was the moment when the last part of my childhood slipped away forever. However this turned out, I would never forgive my parents. It was possible I would understand them, maybe even sympathise with them from time to time. But I would never truly forgive them. The realisation tasted bitter.

Mum suddenly pulled back the bedclothes and Dad increased his grip on me, tried to sit me up, get me out of bed. I think they'd decided I was hysterical and were trying to force me to pay attention. Maybe they were just going to shut me down there and then. But if they were thinking hysteria, I'd show them. I'd show them proper hysteria.

I twisted out of Dad's grasp and it was surprisingly easy. I think I was in the grip of a huge adrenaline rush and I felt strong. I felt so strong. I butted him in the stomach and I heard the wind rush out of his lungs. He doubled over and I ran for the door, turned the handle and nearly got away, but Mum grabbed me from behind and dragged me a little way back into the room. I screamed and jabbed my elbow back, making contact with some part of her body. I heard her gasp and then I was free. This time I ran as fast as I could. Behind me I heard a shout of 'Get him. Don't let him get away.'

I ran down a number of corridors, taking turns at random. Once I turned a corner and a middle-aged man in a white coat was a metre ahead of me. I caught him a glancing blow and then I was in clear space once more. I ran and ran, checking my internal clock. Three and a half minutes. Maybe. Aiden should have pressed the emergency override by now. He couldn't do it right outside the gate, because that would make his recapture easier when Mum called the security guards to search the area. Had I told him that? I didn't think I had. Hopefully, he'd worked that out for himself. So, if everything had gone well, he'd be a minute and a half away from the lab, the car door would be open and he'd run into the rain and the wind, and the darkness would give him shelter. Maybe.

I had no idea where I was, but I turned another corner and the lab entrance was in front of me. I burst through the doors, but nearly didn't make it. I don't know where Dad came from, but his hand grabbed the shoulder of Aiden's nightclothes, so I twisted and felt the fabric rip. Then I was in the storm and I couldn't see a thing. The rain was so intense that visibility was reduced to no more than two metres. In less than a second I was as drenched as if I'd dived into our pool at home. I had to buy some more time and maybe the storm could be my friend. I ran with no idea where I was going.

The storm wasn't my friend. I ran straight into a security guard, who caught me in a grip I knew I would never break. This guy was strong. I stopped struggling and went limp instead. He half-dragged, half-carried me back into the lab. Judging by his muttering he wasn't very pleased that I'd caused him to get soaked. I didn't care. Over four minutes. He *must* be away by now.

Mum and Dad had the guard carry me into another room, where a nurse strapped me to a bed. The friendly 'call-me-Sue', I assumed. She didn't seem that friendly to me. Another man came into the room, the one I'd side-swiped in my race around the building. He didn't appear that friendly either. It occurred to me that at the first sign of a hypodermic needle, I'd have to speak up. It wouldn't be the best outcome to save Aiden's life while losing my own. I love my brother, but...

That wasn't necessary. Mum dried my face with a towel, pushed my wet hair back from my forehead. And then her eyes widened and I knew she knew.

Almost immediately, she took out her tablet and punched in instructions. You didn't have to be a genius to work out that she was recalling the car. I thought I'd bought Aiden enough time, but I couldn't be sure. If he hadn't pressed the emergency stop, he'd presumably do so when the car turned around. Then again, knowing Mum's expertise, she was probably able to disarm that function remotely.

'What are you doing, Chrissie?' asked Dad.

Mum didn't answer. Instead she stood over me.

'Where's he gone, Ashleigh?'

'Somewhere you'll never find him,' I replied. I could see Dad's face over Mum's shoulder. Judging by his expression, the penny had dropped with him as well.

'I wouldn't be too sure of that,' Mum replied. She said that with such confidence that instantly I became scared again. I'd been feeling happy, so happy at the thought he'd escaped. Yes, I was waiting to see an empty car return before I really started celebrating, but now I wondered if Mum *could* track him down. I hadn't thought that through but it occurred to me that she might well have put a transmitter somewhere into his body. They used to do that to track animals. Mum would always want to know where her creation was. I felt like crying.

'Unstrap her,' said Mum to the nurse.

Call-me-Sue also found some dry clothes, so I was able to watch the car drive up to the door. It was empty. Then I did allow myself to celebrate a little. Even if Mum was able to track him, it didn't mean she could necessarily bring him in. It's a lawless world out there and Aiden is smart and Aiden is tough.

We went home and Mum said nothing on the drive back. It was obvious she was thinking and that worried me. My mother is the smartest person I have ever known and she wasn't panicking. She was working through a problem, step by step. It's what she had done her entire life and she was very good at it. The lifestyle we enjoyed was evidence of that.

I took some bread and cheese from the fridge and shut myself away in my bedroom. No one stopped me. Mum had gone straight to her office. Dad looked lost. I put the chair under the doorhandle again before getting my tablet from under the bed and calling Aiden. I was hoping that in the confusion of the escape, Mum hadn't thought

I might have smuggled in Aiden's tablet and that we could be in communication. She'd work it out eventually, but I had some time on my side. I hoped.

Aiden answered immediately.

'What the hell is going on, Ash?' he said. Under other circumstances I'd have been tempted to cry. His hologram, wearing that yellow dress (a small part of me noticed the headband had gone), was shivering, a tiny Z hugged close.

'Are you safe?' I said.

'No. I'm cold and wet and lost. It's dark and I'm scared and I want to come home.'

My heart lurched, but I couldn't let pity be his downfall.

'Listen to me, Aiden,' I said. 'You *mustn't* come home. If you do, you'll die. Please trust me on this. And whatever you do, don't talk to Mum and Dad. Find Xena and her gang if you can. She said she likes you and I think they may protect you.'

He started crying then and that got me going. He seemed so lost and small and helpless.

'I don't understand anything,' he sobbed.

'I'll be at the entrance of Victoria Park at nine in the morning,' I said, without having the slightest idea how I was going to manage that. 'Stay hidden and only come out if I'm alone. Do you understand?'

'Yes, but…'

'Find shelter, but keep moving. Don't call me back and don't stay in the same place for too long. I'll explain everything tomorrow, Aiden. I swear.' I hung up. I didn't want to, but I needed him scared and jumpy. For a while, at least, I thought his survival would depend on it.

I'll explain everything tomorrow? I'd have to do that. But that didn't mean I was looking forward to it.

I'm not sure if anyone slept that night. I know I didn't, and judging by the faces of my parents in the morning, they hadn't either. It was certain Aiden hadn't got any rest, but his absence and Mum's presence was evidence he hadn't been recaptured. Not conclusive, but…

Mum pretty much confirmed that hope by speaking on her tablet almost continuously. She kept away from me, but I heard the occasional word and I thought she was organising a search. Then she called for the car.

'We will talk about this, Ashleigh,' she said as she was walking through the front door. They were the first words she'd said to me since we were in the lab. 'When this problem is sorted – and it *will* be sorted – we will be having a full and frank discussion.'

I thought of saying something sharp, but decided silence would serve me better. I watched as the car drove her away.

Just me and Dad.

I looked at him across the kitchen table. He seemed to have aged years in just a few hours. He plucked at his earlobe and there was a twitch under his right eye. He tried to smile at me but that didn't work.

'Call the car, Dad,' I said after five minutes. We had three cars. I have no idea why, since the three hadn't ever been on the road at the same time.

'Why? Where are we going, Ash?'

'To see Aiden,' I said. That got his full attention. His eyes flicked to one side, where his tablet lay. 'I can't stop you ringing Mum,' I continued, 'but if you do, you won't see him and I will never tell you where he is. So you need to make a decision, Dad. For once.'

I think he flinched at that. Our eyes met and neither of us broke contact. I don't know if it was wishful thinking, but I thought I saw a determination in his eyes – a kind of flintiness – that hadn't been there before. Then he nodded slowly.

'Let's go,' he said.

I made Dad park the car at the school, which was deserted for the holidays. We were going to walk from there.

He didn't look comfortable as we headed down an empty street. I wondered when he'd last walked the streets of Sydney. It must have been a long time ago, judging by his nervousness and how he kept spinning around as if expecting to be attacked from every quarter. I was slightly more relaxed. I'd done this twice before, though it was still a bit scary. When we arrived at Victoria Park I pulled out my tablet and called Aiden. He answered immediately.

'I'm here, Aiden,' I said. 'And Dad is with me.'

I could tell Aiden was confused and I could understand why. I'd told him to avoid our parents and now I'd brought one along. This wouldn't be making any sense to him. But I'd taken a chance with Dad. I'd made him leave his tablet on the kitchen table because I didn't trust him *too* much, but I also thought that, away from Mum, he might have his own ideas and opinions. And he couldn't do much out here. Aiden could outrun most people. He could certainly outrun Dad.

'I'll leave Dad at the entrance arch,' I said. 'He won't be coming to talk to you. That's just me. If he does try to approach you, stay out of his way. Run if you have to. But I don't think he will, I think he's got more sense than that.' I hoped so, but I couldn't guarantee it. 'I'll walk in a couple of hundred metres to where the park is emptiest. Meet me there.' I wanted plenty of room, so that we could see if anyone or anything approached. 'You *are* here, aren't you, Aiden?'

'I'm here.'

'Good. I'm walking now.'

I hung up and turned to Dad. 'Stay here. Any move and we'll both be gone. I'm having a conversation with my brother. After that, he may want to talk to you. Then again, he may not. Either way, we'll respect his wishes.'

Dad just nodded. He looked worried and scared and defeated all at the same time. That suited me. That's exactly how I wanted him to be. I turned and headed into the park.

The sun was already intense and the humidity was off the scale, a consequence of last night's storm, which was severe even by Sydney standards. I wiped sweat from my forehead and scanned the park. I didn't see Aiden until I'd stopped in the very middle of a clearing, the nearest tree maybe sixty or seventy metres away. He stepped out from behind one of them and started walking towards me. I was expecting to see the yellow dress, but he had different clothes on. Maybe he'd stolen some... but then I saw Xena and a couple of her gang appear from behind neighbouring trees. She held Zorro in her arms and watched as my brother approached me. He'd found them. They'd given him clothing and shelter. I felt one worry melt away. Trouble was, there were so many others and they were solid and enduring.

Aiden stopped a metre away. He glanced over my shoulder, checking out Dad, I guessed. He seemed in much better shape this morning. When I'd rung last night he'd been tearful, on the verge of a breakdown. Now he was... cool. Thinking. Analysing. It was better this way.

I pointed over his shoulder. 'You should tell Xena and the others that they need to find another activity. Standing around looking threatening is getting a bit old.'

Aiden didn't smile.

'I thought all this might have been some elaborate sibling joke, Ash,' he said. 'But Dad is behind you, so I guess he puts paid to that idea.'

'I wish it was a joke. It isn't.'

'So tell me.'

And I did. I told him as simply and as clearly as I could. He deserved that. He deserved a whole lot more, but the only thing I could give him now was the plain truth, plainly told. My voice didn't break and when I was done I was surprised to find tears running down my cheeks. I couldn't remember when I'd started crying.

Aiden didn't flinch and his expression didn't change. He listened until all my words had dried up. Then he reached out a hand and brushed away a tear from my cheek.

'Wait here for me, Ash,' he said. 'Please.'

And he walked away. Not towards Xena and the others but towards a rotting bench on the edge of the clearing. In the Sydney of old, people would've sat there, enjoying the day, enjoying the trees and the way sunshine filtered through leaves. Now Aiden sat, back straight, head not moving, as if carved from the same wood.

I waited. I waited for an hour. My legs were trembling but I didn't want to sit on the grass, and not just because it was still wet from the storm. I wanted to be solid for Aiden. Unmoving. There. Never flinching.

Finally, he stood and walked back. I still couldn't read anything in his expression.

'Call Dad over,' he said. 'I want to talk to him.'

I turned. Dad was sitting against the entrance wall, almost exactly where Xena had sat all that time ago. I waved and he stood. He walked slowly towards us, like someone approaching the unknown. Careful. Scared. Dad stopped a couple of steps away. His mouth opened and then it closed. I imagine he'd searched his brain for a suitable greeting but had come up with nothing. I was glad.

Aiden reached into his pocket, pulled out his tablet and unfolded it. He punched in a command and then handed it to Dad.

'I need to talk to both of you,' he said.

Mum's face appeared on the screen. Dad held it so we could see. In fact he held it so his face and Mum's were pretty much side by side. Maybe he was relieved that Mum was there. She was always better with words. Now he didn't have to bother. I took a step to stand next to my brother. If Mum was surprised by what she saw, she didn't give anything away.

'Hello, Aiden,' she said.

'Hello, Mum.'

'Ashleigh has told you, I assume?'

Aiden nodded.

'Okay, Aiden. I want you to listen very carefully to what I'm about to say.' Mum's voice. Patient. Reasonable. 'You have always been very logical, so I want you to think through all the implications of the situation we find ourselves in. I did not want this to happen. I imagined us all growing old together as a family. You wouldn't have been able to have children, obviously. But Ashleigh could. I had a vision of us all, three generations, looking out for each other. Protecting each other. It was really that simple.'

'Not so simple now,' said Aiden.

Mum nodded. 'Not simple at all. And I confess that's my fault. I didn't take enough care. I had a vision. Passing on our wealth to you, Ashleigh and maybe her future partner and child. I did it all for love.'

'Did you love me, Mamma?' Aiden's voice, still calm. 'Am I alive and did you love me?'

For the briefest moment, Mum's composure cracked and slid. Her mouth twisted and I thought I saw pain and the faintest shimmer of tears in her eyes. Then she shuddered and glanced down, and when she lifted her face to the screen once more she was calm, her eyes dry. I thought I'd seen something buried within, struggling to find the surface, but it might have been my imagination. Her voice didn't waver when she replied.

'You're a machine, Aiden. You were never alive.'

I was desperate to say something, but I bit my tongue. This was between them and I had no right to speak. But I had to hand it to my mother. She wasn't going to sugar-coat anything, say stuff just to make anyone feel good. Maybe including herself. It was almost admirable. Almost. But she'd avoided one question.

'So you aren't going to kill me, is that right?' said Aiden. 'Just shut me down. Because you can't kill something that isn't alive.'

'That's correct.'

'You didn't answer my first question. Did you ever love me?'

'*I* did.' I'd almost forgotten Dad was still there. Mum's face and the intensity of her words had made him fade into the background. It often happened like that. 'And I still do,' he continued. 'I love you, Aiden.'

My brother nodded. Mum stayed silent.

'Do you know something?' I said. 'I look from you, Mum, to my brother and I think I know which one is the machine.'

She didn't say anything to that. Instead she fixed her eyes on Aiden once more.

'If you ever loved Ashleigh, Aiden, you will hand yourself over to me. You may not know it, you may not *feel* it, but you are out of control. Your mind is behaving in ways that were never intended. Left unchecked, you are a danger not just to Ash, but to everyone. I want you to think carefully about this and make the right decision. It's just logic, Aiden. Put emotions to one side for a moment. Think this through.'

'I'm thinking,' said Aiden.

'I will track you down,' Mum continued. 'If you don't do the right thing, I will have to find you and make you do it. You know me, Aiden. I don't say I will do something if I can't. I have resources. You're on your own.'

'He's not on his own,' I said.

'No,' said Mum. 'You have Ashleigh and my husband on your side, apparently. That's not going to be enough. I have the means and I *will* find you.'

'I believe you,' said Aiden. 'You always kept your promises, Mamma. Goodbye.' And he turned and walked away.

I ran after him.

'Aiden,' I said. 'I'm coming with you. I'll just get your tablet back and then I'll come with you.'

'I don't want the tablet,' said Aiden. He stopped walking. 'It's not really going to be much use to me.' He cupped my face in his hands. 'And you *can't* come with me, Ash. She's right about a few things. I have always protected you and the only way I can do that now is to ask you to go back home with Dad. He needs you and he'll look after you. Where I'm going, you'll just be something else I have to worry about.'

I stamped my feet. It was childish, but it felt good.

'Can everyone stop being so freaking logical?' I asked. 'Just for one moment. I *am* coming with you. You're my brother.'

He gave a half-smile, examined my face. Then he nodded.

'One night, Ashleigh. Promise me that tomorrow you'll go home. If you can't do that, then I'll just run away, here and now. You'll never be able to catch me.'

'No,' I replied. 'I couldn't. But that wouldn't stop me trying. And then I'd be all alone in Sydney with no one to protect me. And then you'd have to come back. So admit defeat, Aiden. You were never as smart as me.'

There was that hint of a smile again.

'One night, Ash. Promise.'

I looked into his eyes and for a moment thought I saw the speed with which his thoughts were turning. I didn't think he needed me anymore. But I needed him, and I had to take whatever I could.

'I promise.'

I ran back to Dad.

'Have the car wait for me here at ten o'clock tomorrow morning,' I said. He'd shut down Aiden's tablet. I handed him mine. 'Just so no one gets in touch,' I said. *Just so no one can track my whereabouts*, I thought. 'I'm spending time with my brother. Your son.'

And Dad just nodded. Smiled and put a hand to my cheek.

'Take care,' he said. 'Both of you.'

'I'll tell Mum you couldn't stop me,' I said.

'That's okay,' he said. 'I think it's time I told her some things of my own.'

17

Xena passed Zorro over to Aiden and then fell into step with me.

'Can't get rid of you guys,' she said. 'No offence, but you're like a bad smell.'

'Thank you for helping my brother,' I replied.

She laughed. 'Hey. An accident. We're going through an underpass after the storm and found this shivering… *mess* in a yellow dress, of all things. Holding a dog. I felt bad for the dog, not for the mess in the dress. I'd've just taken the dog but I couldn't split him from the freak in yellow, so no choice. Amazing how they perked up after a spell in front of a fire. Even tried to feed 'em, but I guess they weren't hungry.'

'Thank you.'

We walked in silence for a couple of minutes. The park was behind us now and we were travelling through deserted streets. Aiden walked ahead, chatting with Ziggy.

They seemed to have forgotten their differences, judging by the way Ziggy was smiling at something Aiden was saying.

'Where are we going?' I asked.

'Headquarters,' said Xena. 'A house a few streets away.'

'Headquarters of what?'

Xena looked at me, shook her head and smiled.

'I'd forgotten you don't know nothing,' she said. 'The rich kid. Why should you know? Tell me something, princess…'

'Stop calling me that,' I said, 'or I'll punch your lights out. My name is Ashleigh.'

She stopped and laughed. She laughed so hard that she had to bend over double. Everyone stopped and looked back at her. It took a minute for her to recover and when she did, she waved a hand at the group. We started moving again.

'Sorry, Ashleigh,' said Xena, still smiling. 'Us women shouldn't put each other down. We've got enough problems with men doing it. Anyway, I was goin' to ask. What's your place like, eh? Tell me about where you live.'

'I don't want to talk about it.'

'Big place, I reckon. Lotsa security. Your own gardens, so you grow craploads of veggies. Solar sail covering the roof – am I right? Plenty of shade *and* plenty of electricity. Maybe you sell some of the juice you can't use to any poor people around. If you've *got* any poor people around.'

'No underprivileged people around *us*,' I said. 'And you forgot our swimming pool. But, other than that…'

Xena stopped and whistled.

'A pool? Wow. We hit the motherlode with you guys. Maybe I should take Ziggy's advice. Ransom you, not your brother there. Can't imagine he's keen to go home since he ran away in a yellow dress. What ya reckon your folks would pay to get *you* back, Ashleigh?'

'More than you can imagine,' I said.

'Doubt it,' said Xena. 'I've got a helluvan imagination.'

'So you've got me stereotyped,' I said. 'What about you? Dirty. Will kill anything that moves. Not bothered about improving the world, just taking what you can. Am I close?'

She laughed again. Xena laughed a lot, I was beginning to realise.

'Pretty close,' she replied. 'Dirty, yup. Kill anything that moves, nah. You're still here. For now. Taking what we can, sure. No one gives us *anything*, prin...Ashleigh. What we got, we've had to get ourselves.'

'Headquarters?' We seemed to have moved away from the topic.

'Ah, yeah. Now, no offence, but I'm gonna assume you know nothing, okay?'

'Assume away.'

'Right. So there're three sections to society. Four, if you count the poor wandering buggers who're even worse off than us. The top band – people like you. The ones with wealth and power. In control. The kind of people who screwed over the planet in the first place and then, when it all turned to crap, kept control anyway.'

'But…'

Xena held up her hand.

'Second, the people who work for those of you in the top band, keeping you safe and comfortable and, most importantly, still in power. The doctors, the nurses, the scientists, the teachers, the builders. But most of all, the security. Eighty per cent of people with jobs work in the security area. Did you know that?' She laughed again. 'Hey, dumb me, huh? Why *would* you know? That's all way beneath you.'

We turned a corner. Everyone appeared to relax a little, as if somehow the environment was safer. I couldn't see any change from one street to another, but shoulders seemed looser. Kids took their hands from the handles of their knives. They didn't glance around as much.

'These're the people,' Xena continued, 'who live in the gated settlements. People who live by the laws, who get food delivered to them, who've got solar panels for lighting, heating and air conditioning. If they're lucky, mind. Sometimes those things don't happen, but what are you gonna do, huh? Who do you complain to? They're also the people who have one child and that's it. Pop out one, you get your bits seen to. Their communities are guarded. I mean, *seriously* guarded.'

I thought of Charlotte and her parents, working all the hours they could to protect their standing in their community. I imagined my friend poring over her schoolwork for hour upon countless hour, determined not just to protect what she had, but to climb further up the ladder, to become one of the ruling class by dint of willpower, education and a self-discipline I couldn't begin to comprehend. It wasn't just ambition that motivated her, I suddenly realised, but also fear. Fear of slipping from their nice house to just another ordinary one in the community and from there to one close to the walls and the warning sirens and from there to outside the gate and therefore beyond protection, becoming...

Xena snapped her fingers in front of my eyes.

'Earth to Ashleigh,' she said. 'Are you receiving me?'

'Sorry,' I said. 'I was thinking about a friend. You were saying? The people in the communities are guarded. They're guarded from...'

'From us,' said Xena. 'The final tier. The outcasts. We're the ones who don't fit into the top two levels. The ones who *can't* get a job in security. Or choose not to. The ones who're free to live however we want. So we forage, we barter, we trade for everything, look after our own little... you'd probably call it a tribe. We say family.'

She pointed to a large house with a massive gate and a high fence surrounding it. It was about a hundred metres ahead on the right of the road.

'Headquarters,' she said. 'Where the leaders care for our people. This district is ours. Other districts belong to other families. We defend our territory, they defend theirs. And then, of course, there're the people who don't belong anywhere. The wanderers. Now they're *really* a worry. Especially if you bump into one on a dark night.'

'This is what you talked to my brother about? That day in the park.'

'Among other things. He wasn't as...ignorant as you, but he sure had a lot to learn.'

I nodded. I was beginning to realise that despite my expensive education, maybe *because* of my expensive education, I knew virtually nothing at all. As if to prove the point, the closer we got to Xena's Headquarters, the more baffled I became.

'What is that noise and what is that disgusting smell?' I asked.

Xena appeared genuinely puzzled.

'That squealing,' I added. It was like metal scraping along metal, the kind of high-pitched noise that sets your teeth on edge and feels like pain against the temples.

She laughed. 'Oh, *that* noise. *That* smell. Pigs. Dozens of 'em. We keep 'em round the back. Their crap's no good for the vegetables, but we compost it down. Couple of months it's okay to use.'

'You put up with that noise and smell for *compost*?'

'Nah. We put up with it for bacon.'

'Isn't bacon a type of meat?'

Xena laughed again. I was apparently a source of considerable amusement for her and it was getting irritating. 'Oh, yeah. Oh, yeah. OH, YEAH! Only the best meat in the whole freakin' world.'

'You people eat *meat*?' I thought back to Charlotte. She brought beef sandwiches to school, but she didn't eat them. I think they were fake beef anyway. Like that chicken substitute her mother served us at her house. I suspected Charlotte only did it to impress. If that was the case, I didn't know *anyone* who ate meat. Until now.

'What else are you gonna do with it?' said Xena. 'Do they teach you nothing at that fancy school? Come on, girl. Let's go in. I'll introduce you to Nonna.'

Ziggy opened a padlock on the front gate and we all trooped through. The house seemed normal, though it could've done with a good coat of paint and some of the wood on the window frames was rotting and flaking. But the smell was making my eyes water, so I couldn't take in too many details. Xena led me up the porch steps, through the open front door, into a long, dark corridor and then into what was obviously a kitchen. An old, large woman was at a central bench doing something with flour. She looked up, saw us and smiled.

'Who have we here?' she said. Her accent was strange. I couldn't place it.

'This here's Ashleigh,' said Xena. 'Sister of the boy we picked up last night. And this here's Nonna.'

'Pleased to meet you,' I said.

'And pleased to meet you, Ashleigh,' said Nonna. She came over and gave me a big hug, which took me by surprise. A cloud of flour exploded behind my back and when she pulled away I sneezed. Nonna laughed. 'Are you looking to stay with us?'

'Just one night. If that's all right,' I said.

'Of course. We've no spare beds but if you don't mind the floor, I'm sure we can find a blanket or two for you.'

'Thank you.'

She picked up a huge ball of dough and started kneading it on the floury counter. 'What do you say to pizza for dinner?' she asked. 'With tomatoes straight off the vine, onions, home-made goat's cheese and stacks of ham.'

I looked to Xena for help, but she just laughed at me.

'I don't know what ham is,' I admitted. 'But, yes. Please. Thank you.'

'Ham's a rare vegetable,' said Xena. 'You'll love it.' But she could hardly stop laughing. Nonna frowned and wagged a finger in her direction.

'That is very wrong of you, Lauren, and you know it.' She turned to me. 'Ham is a cut of meat from a pig, Ashleigh.'

'I don't eat meat,' I said. 'I think it's wrong...I mean, I was *brought up* to think it's wrong. I don't mean you...'

'I'll make you some pizza with just vegetables,' said Nonna. 'Take no notice of Lauren's teasing. Are you okay with cheese, though?'

'Oh, yes,' I said. 'Thank you, Nonna. And thank you...Lauren.'

It wasn't a friendly glare I got this time.

'Okay, clear off, the pair of you. I'm cooking for nearly a hundred people tonight and I can't afford to waste time chatting. Lauren, I'm using up all the ham – we need to set some more curing. Go on. Run along and give me space.'

'Come on, Ashleigh,' said Xena. 'I'll introduce you to our pigs. They've never met a rich kid before, but they're not too fussy about who they hang with, so you'll be right.'

It was all I could do not to puke. I couldn't stop the gagging, though.

The pigs, about fifteen of them, were running around in a wooden enclosure with what appeared to be mud for a floor. On closer examination it seemed to be a combination of mud and manure. I gagged again. Xena didn't seem bothered in the slightest. She leaned against a fence and looked over the squirming mass of pink flesh with what seemed like affection.

'Eight piglets,' she said. 'And more on the way when that sow over there farrows.' I had no idea what she was talking about – more confirmation, if it was needed, of my ignorance. 'Any of those piglets take your fancy, Ashleigh?'

'They're all revolting.'

'No. They're not. Pigs are actually really smart. They've got an amazing sense of smell, too.'

'They must be really suffering living next to each other, then.'

Xena laughed. 'Let's look at Babe here.' She opened a gate and grabbed a piglet as it tried to squirm away. Despite myself, I was impressed. Xena's reaction speed was incredible and the piglet was no slouch either, but in one smooth movement she had it firmly in her arms.

'You give the pigs names?' I said.

'Nah. I call 'em all Babe. Simpler that way.' She hugged the piglet close to her and latched the gate again. 'Say hello to Ashleigh, Babe,' she said, bringing the thing up towards my face. I backed away.

What happened next was so fast and so unexpected that it took me several seconds just to process it. Xena's hand moved up and across and a fountain of red arced towards me, splashing the front of my T-shirt. I flinched and turned my face away but not before I felt droplets, warm and burning, against my cheeks. When I turned back, Xena was holding the piglet upside down by its trotters. Blood ran, a thick stream, from its neck, pooling into the dirt. The piglet spasmed a couple of times and stilled. Even then, I didn't really understand what had just happened. I put a hand up to my face and it came away red.

It was then I screamed. I think it was then. But whenever it was, it was difficult to stop.

Xena slapped me across the face, at least once, but maybe twice. Hard.

'What the hell's wrong with you?' she yelled. I don't know if it was the shouting or the slap, but I suddenly found my screams had jammed in my throat.

'You killed that pig,' I whispered. 'You cut its throat.'

She glanced down at the body she still held. A knife, red and dripping, was clenched in her grip, its blade snug against the animal's legs.

'Course I did,' she said. 'How else was it gonna die? Of harsh words and a broken heart?'

'You murdered it.'

She put her face even closer to mine. Instinctively I took a step back.

'Are you crazy?' she hissed. 'Murder? Murder is what happens when your parents are stopped in the street and beaten to death for nothing more than the clothes on their backs. Murder is when one of *your* fancy hospitals turns away one of my people and leaves him to die in the road like a dog. Because the drugs that could've cured him are kept for the likes of you and your parents. Murder is when...' She took a deep breath and turned away. She wiped her forehead with a blood-stained arm, dropped her head and stood still for a moment. When Xena turned back to me, her eyes had lost some of their fire.

'Sorry,' she said. She took another breath. 'I should've guessed you'd react that way.' She glanced down at the body in her hand. 'I slaughtered this pig as quickly as I could. They're not pets, they're food. I made it as painless as possible. I...' She shook her head. 'Your brother is here,' she continued. She gave a nod over my left shoulder. 'Go talk to him. I have to gut and clean this animal and I don't think you wanna be around for that. Go talk to your brother. And I *am* sorry, Ashleigh. I didn't think and I should've done.'

18

Without my tablet I had no way of telling the time, but judging by the position of the sun it was around midday. Aiden and I sat at a picnic table. It was old and splintered and had benches along two sides. There was a hole in the centre with a battered umbrella stuck into it and that gave a little bit of shade. It was hot, but I liked that no one was fussing about sunblock and UV levels. We kept in the shade, though. Stupid not to.

I felt a little better. Aiden had helped me clean up a bit, though my T-shirt was still stained. At least my face, he assured me, was blood-free.

'I feel stupid,' I said.

'No. Not stupid, Ashleigh. We have led particularly sheltered lives, you and me. It's not our fault that we have little experience of … life's nastier sides. And you had no idea it was going to happen.'

'I should've, though, Aiden. I should've. Nonna told Xena to prepare some ham. And that's what she did. But I...'

Aiden put his hand on mine. I had been plucking at a few of the splinters in the wood, trying to prise them loose.

'It's been a stressful few days,' he said. 'Hey, how's that for understatement?' I gave a tired smile. 'So cut yourself some slack,' he continued.

'I'll try,' I said.

We sat in silence for a few minutes, lost in our own thoughts. When I glanced up, Aiden was staring at the sky, one hand absent-mindedly scratching Z, who lay panting on the bench next to him.

'What are you thinking about?' I asked.

He smiled and pointed upwards.

'Do you see them, Ashleigh?'

I squinted, but there was nothing there as far as I could tell. Then again, the sun was too bright and painful and I couldn't look for long. The glare didn't appear to bother Aiden.

'What?'

'Drones,' he said. 'Mother's drones, watching us.'

I immediately tensed.

'She knows where we are?'

'She *always* knows where we are, Ash. There's nothing we can do about that.'

Leaving my tablet behind, it turned out, was completely pointless. 'Then she'll be sending people to get you,' I said. Another thought immediately crossed my mind, one even more worrying. 'You don't think those drones could hurt you, do you?' It would be simple for Mum to arm a drone, program it to select a specific target. She could do it without breaking a sweat.

'No. She couldn't risk a strike, especially while you're here.'

'Then I'll stay with you all the time.'

'But even when you've gone, she won't. Mum might be all sorts of things, but there are people around and she won't take the risk that someone could be hurt by being close to me. She's not a killer.'

'She wants to kill you.'

'But I'm not a person. You have to see things from her perspective.'

I snorted. 'No, I don't. Anyway, she could still be sending someone.'

Aiden shook his head.

'Same reason. Security guards are people. They would probably refuse to come into a place like this because it's too dangerous and Mum wouldn't ask them to come here because it could mean their death. Our friends here are hospitable, but they can be ruthless in defence of their land and their people.'

'Then you're safe here.'

'Nope.' Aiden picked up Z and put him on the table between us. The dog immediately sat and looked at my brother with eyes full of worship and a tongue that drooped and lolled.

'I don't understand.'

'Here's what I'd do in her place,' said Aiden. 'I'd produce some bots, small bots like insects. Maybe make them look *exactly* like insects. Send a swarm, all of them programmed to find me, bite me, put something into my system that would...well, would achieve what she wants to achieve.'

'Could she do that?'

Aiden played with Z's ear. 'For someone who could make this, let alone make me, it would be very simple engineering.'

I felt like crying. It sounded hopeless.

'So what are you going to do?'

'I'm going to use my strengths. And I think I have many, probably more than I realise...'

I remembered what Mum had said about the necessity of killing my brother, how he would turn into something that could threaten the survival of the whole human race. And so I told him. I told him about Stephen Hawking and the idea that an AI using a deep neural network could produce ever more sophisticated and efficient versions of itself, to the point that no human could ever be an intellectual match. That such a being might condense millions of years of evolution into minutes, hours or seconds.

Aiden let me speak, nodding occasionally, but I could tell he was only partially listening. His mind was racing ahead, taking the information, processing it, analysing it and exploring all the possibilities it contained. Maybe I hadn't told him anything he hadn't already considered.

After a while I dribbled to a stop. Aiden kept thinking, staring off into the distance, his hand still rubbing Z under his chin.

And then I started to worry. What had Mum said to me? We'd have no idea what he might turn into but it probably wouldn't be the brother I'd always known. Was I even now watching Aiden leaving me?

He smiled.

'I've been very lucky,' he said. 'That limiter Mum installed in my brain. It was obviously damaged in the kayak accident. When it wasn't working properly, I started to have … well, such strange thoughts, Ash. You remember. You were worried I was turning weird. But in fact they were just my intellectual baby steps. I saw things clearly. I saw … connections. I felt there was no problem I couldn't solve. But that scared me and I tried to shut it down. Now I know that was a mistake.'

'Can I ask you something?'

'Of course.'

'In the park I told you that you're not human. You didn't break down, you didn't tell me I was lying, you didn't even argue. Instead, you walked away for an hour, came back and it was like you'd accepted everything. That's just … just …'

'Not a normal human reaction?'

'Exactly.' Aiden smiled and then I understood what he was getting at. 'Oh, I see.'

'You said I was away for an hour, Ashleigh. For me it felt like days, weeks even. Something is happening with time.'

He tapped his head. 'Up here. I'm thinking and feeling quicker and quicker. Having this conversation...well, it's kind of like wading through mud. I speak a sentence, but a million others go through my head in the time it takes me to say it. It's scary and amazing all at the same time.'

'You're doing what Mum said you'd do. You're evolving into...something else.'

Aiden reached across the table and took my hand.

'I said before that I tried to shut things down, banish the ideas I was getting, become...more normal, I suppose. I think the news you gave me wasn't really news at all, Ash. I think I knew the truth, somewhere in my...what's the right expression? Memories? Algorithm pathways? And the knowledge that I am a machine has given me permission to behave like a machine. I'm discovering stuff about myself all the time. It's like before I was operating at one thousandth of one per cent of my capacity.' He laughed. 'Charlotte would be impressed.'

'I don't want you to change into something else,' I said. 'I want you to stay my brother.' I could feel tears gathering. I didn't want to cry, not on what was probably going to be our last day together for a long time. Maybe forever. Aiden squeezed my hand harder.

'I think whatever I change into, I will always be your brother, Ash.'

'You think. You don't know.'

'No,' he said. 'I don't know.'

At first I thought the dinner must have been some kind of birthday party. As darkness gathered, four or five people carried in a piano, of all things. Others set up barbecues and made firepits, brought in dozens of old-style plastic chairs. One old man played the piano and then a couple of girls brought out violins and accompanied him on them.

Over the next few hours nearly a hundred people turned up. There was dancing and laughter and everyone seemed to be having a good time.

At one point, Nonna came and sat beside me.

'Having fun?' she asked.

'Oh, yes,' I said. 'Just like everyone else. Is it someone's birthday?'

She laughed.

'Not quite,' she said. 'It's a wake.'

I didn't really know what to say. What was awake? I didn't want to ask. These people probably already thought I was a total moron. But Nonna must have read the incomprehension in my face.

'A wake is a celebration when someone has died,' she said. 'It's a celebration of the life they've lived and the mark they've made on the world.'

I tried to get my head around this. From my limited experience, death was normally accompanied by the sadness of those who survive. Yet when I thought about it a little more, I could see the point of celebration. If I was dead I'd rather someone was happy I'd lived, than just sad I'd died. Of course, a bit of sadness would be in order...

'I'm sorry,' I said. 'Was it someone close to you?'

'He was close to all of us,' Nonna replied. 'There's a good reason why we call our community a family.'

'I'm sorry.'

'You get used to it, unfortunately,' she said. 'If we had more access to medicines and basic medical care, then deaths wouldn't be so common. But now sicknesses that even two hundred years ago were survivable can, and do, take us off.' She shook her head. 'Enough of this talk. I didn't come here to make you gloomy. I came to give you these.' She reached into her pocket and brought out a watch and a ring, thrust them into my hand. 'Lauren told me these belonged to your parents. I'd be grateful if you took them back.'

'But Nonna,' I said. 'These are very valuable. You should keep them. It won't make any difference to my parents but it could buy you all sorts of amazing things.'

Nonna laughed.

'And what could we buy with money, Ashleigh?'

'Those drugs you were talking about. Medicines. Medical care.'

She shook her head.

'Those things are not for sale. At least not to the likes of us. They're reserved for the people with power. True, they're normally also the ones with money. But we are disposable. To be honest, every time one of us dies, those in power see it as one problem less. There's no incentive, at least in their minds, to keep us alive.'

'You must hate us,' I said.

'Why would I? There's no profit in hate.'

I turned the watch and the ring over in my hands.

'Why did Xena … Lauren take these then, if they aren't of use?'

'That girl! She likes shiny things. And she knew *you* thought they were important. But they're not. They're really not.' Nonna ran a hand through her hair. 'We trade, we barter. If we need something built and no one here can do it, we might trade a pig for someone who can. That's the way our society works. Money is no use if there's nothing to buy. I wouldn't trade that ring in your hand for a pig. You can eat a pig. A ring you can only wear.'

I looked around at all the people, singing, dancing, drinking and eating. I couldn't see Xena anywhere. I put the shiny things into my pocket and felt a bit stupid for having offered them in the first place.

'I think I've upset Xena. Sorry … Lauren,' I said.

'Ah, she told me about your … falling-out. Don't worry. That girl is quick to take offence but she's quicker to forgive and forget. She's got a heart of gold, though she'd punch you in the face if you suggested it.'

'She was so angry when I said she'd murdered that pig.'

'You touched a raw nerve, that's all. Her twin brother died because no one could find the simplest of antibiotics, her parents were murdered in a senseless street attack, her aunt…' Nonna sighed. 'She's seen enough tragedy, that kid, to last a lifetime.'

'Her brother died because all the antibiotics were reserved for my family and people like my family.' I sighed. 'I don't know *how* she can forgive us. I don't know why she doesn't hate us.'

'I told you,' said Nonna. 'There's no profit in it.'

'But there's no loss in it either, sometimes.' The voice came from behind me and it made both Nonna and me jump. I glanced over my shoulder, but the man was already moving around to sit on the bench opposite. His eyes bored into mine and they were hard as stone.

'Micah...' said Nonna.

The man held up a hand but didn't take his eyes off me.

'Not gonna cause trouble, Nonna. Calm down.' He put a mug of something down on the bench. 'Jus' chattin'. See, your little... friend here needs to know not all of us are happy she and her brother are here.' His voice was slightly slurred. 'In fact, some of us are really, really *unhappy*. Know what I mean?'

I didn't know what to say, but it seemed he was expecting some response from me.

'I...'

But he just carried on talking.

'I'll tell you straight. *I* hate you,' he said. 'An' I'm not alone.' He waved a vague hand behind him but still didn't take his eyes from me. 'Plenny o' people here think it's kinda... whass the word? – inappro... *wrong* for you to eat our food, drink our drink when—'

'Micah!' Nonna's hand slammed down on the table so hard a slop of liquid spilled over the edge of the man's mug. 'If you can't behave, you'll have to leave.'

For the first time he glanced at Nonna. He grinned and took a long drink.

'Free speech, Nonna. Free speech. When we stop that?' He picked up the mug, waved it towards me and stood. More drink spilled out. 'You eat our food, we starve,' he said. 'Less be honest here, you doan need nuthin' from us. 'Cause you got it all already, yeah? You got it all and we got nuthin'.'

Nonna stood and the man raised both arms in the air.

'I'm goin',' he said. 'Goin'. But mebbe you should do the same, eh, rich kid. Go. Go back where you come from, while there's still time. Know wha' I mean?'

And he staggered off towards the nearest firepit, slung an arm around another man's shoulder. I put my eyes down. I was scared and I was guilty because a large part of me felt I'd deserved that. Nonna's hand covered mine.

'Take no notice,' she said. 'He's full of it when he's had a few.'

'He's so angry,' I said.

'He's so drunk,' said Nonna.

'But he's also right. I don't belong here. I'm taking but I'm not giving anything back.' I traced a random pattern on the table with a finger. 'I'm leaving tomorrow, but please tell your family that I won't forget what they've done for me and my brother. I *will* give something back to them. I will.' What had Dad said about resigning the househusband role and doing something good for society? Well, I knew where he could make a start.

'Give what you can, take what you need,' said Nonna. 'It's all very simple really.' She patted my hand. 'But don't be scared, Ashleigh. Micah's all bark and no bite. No harm will come to you here. You have my word.'

I felt like crying but I just nodded.

'Speaking of giving something back,' said Nonna, 'those dishes aren't going to wash themselves. Work for food, Ashleigh. The oldest barter of all time. We'll do them together later.'

It was past midnight before I could get to bed and I was exhausted. Xena had found me at one point, grabbed my hands and pulled me to my feet, told me to dance with her. I told her I couldn't dance and she said no one could but that didn't stop them. So I tried. It was fun dancing around the fire but Micah's words had cut and scared me. I kept glancing around but he was nowhere to be seen.

Later I helped with the clearing away and the washing up, something I'd never done in my life. And now I was tired, but it was a tiredness I knew I'd *earned*. When everyone had finally left, Nonna locked the padlock on the front gate and I was able to relax a little. Then she put down some blankets on the living room floor and Aiden and I lay next to each other. It was the hardest bed I'd ever slept on and, in other circumstances, I'd never get a wink of sleep. Tonight I'd probably not even stir.

If I could forget about Micah. So I lay on my back and stared at the ceiling, Aiden's hand in mine. Somewhere, way off in the distance, there was a rumble of thunder. And suddenly I felt a huge surge of déjà vu.

'Remember Queensland, Aiden?' I whispered. 'Holding hands in bed while thunder rattled the windows and the storm had taken out the electricity?'

He chuckled.

'Mamma told us such great stories,' he said. 'And I was all earnest about protecting you if anything should happen and you were such a snotty little kid who felt entitled to that protection.'

'Oi,' I said. 'I might have been a snotty little kid but I was your sister. I still am your sister. Show respect.'

He laughed. When I told him about the confrontation with Micah and the threat he'd made, Aiden simply said he'd be here to protect me until I went home in the morning.

'I'm thinking about the danger to *you*,' I said.

He laughed again. 'Well, to be honest, this Micah guy will have to get to the end of the queue as far as that's concerned. Compared to Mum, I reckon he'll be a pussy cat.'

We were silent for a few minutes. A floorboard creaked above our heads and somewhere someone coughed. Then the house fell silent once more. I could hear Aiden's breathing.

'What are you thinking about, Aiden?'

'Everything,' he said.

'Now who's being snotty?'

'I'm thinking about the way society is structured and how it means the rich get richer and the poor get poorer. I'm thinking about the deaths that have happened and how they could have been prevented. I'm thinking about deaths in the future and how they can be stopped. I'm thinking about climate change, why it occurred and what could be done now to make the planet healthier. I'm thinking about food and how to grow it more efficiently and get it to the people who need it. I'm thinking about humanity expanding into the solar system and beyond, so that human civilisation can go on forever.'

There was silence.

'Among other things,' he added.

I couldn't help it. I laughed out loud and then had to stifle it. Waking people up was no way to show gratitude.

'And here was me thinking you were thinking about important things,' I said. 'You slacker.'

I squeezed his hand.

'All the problems,' I added. 'But have you got the solutions?'

'I think so, yes. To some of them. I'm working on the others.'

'Mum said you wouldn't bother about the problems of humanity if you became a kind of super-being. She said to you our concerns would be trivial.'

'Luckily Mum doesn't know everything. And she seriously under-estimated the bond between brother and sister. If saving you means saving the entire human race, then, hey. I'll give it a go.'

The floorboards beneath me no longer seemed so hard and unforgiving. I could almost feel myself sink into them. Aiden's words were soft and woolly and they were carrying me to sleep.

'You're not a superhero yet, Aiden,' I mumbled. 'Try being a little humble.'

But I'm not sure if I said those words or only thought them. I slept for eight hours straight and I didn't dream.

I said goodbye to Nonna and Xena at Headquarters the next morning. Aiden was going to walk me back to the car, with Ziggy and a couple of the others following for protection. Nonna gave me a big hug. Xena slapped me across the face, but this time it was playful. I *think* it was meant to be playful. To be honest, it hurt a bit. I was sad to go, but I mumbled my goodbyes and took off, Aiden at my side and Zorro trotting at our heels. This wasn't the time to get tearful.

But it was rapidly approaching.

I had so much I wanted to say to my brother, but I was afraid that if I started I would realise that there wasn't the time for it and that would send me into despair. So I plodded along, head down, and tried not to think.

'You seemed to sleep well,' said Aiden.

'I did. You?'

'I didn't sleep,' he said. 'I don't need it anymore, Ash. Maybe I never did. It was just part of a program to shut me down for a time so I was better able to imitate a person. I'm glad that's gone. I need all available time to think, and sleep's a waste.'

'Will you stay here for a while?' I was going to remind him to watch his back.

'No. A day, maybe, and then I'm gone. These people have been good to us and I think the best way to repay them is to move along.'

'Where will you go?'

'I don't know.'

We'd reached the outskirts of Victoria Park. How could we have got here in such a short space of time? It had seemed to take ages going the other way yesterday. I could feel panic bubbling up inside me. How could I say goodbye to my brother?

'Then go somewhere a long way away,' I said. 'Somewhere Mum can't find you.'

'I don't think that's possible. But if there's a way, I'll find it, Ash.'

We stopped in the centre of the park, in the exact spot where I'd told Aiden the truth. Was that only yesterday? Time was playing tricks with me, speeding up and slowing down for no apparent reason. A few hundred metres away was the entrance arch and beyond it, the familiar shape of the car. I didn't want to leave.

Aiden picked up Z and pressed him into my arms.

'Look after him, Ash,' he said.

Now the tears started welling up.

'Aiden ...'

'I'm going now, Ash. I'll have to run because I don't want to be alone for too long. I don't want to be a target. I'll be in touch. Trust me. I *will* contact you. I love you.'

He hugged me. And then he was gone. I watched my brother run towards the trees and I didn't know if I would ever see him again.

I felt broken.

19

THREE MONTHS LATER

Dad knocked on my bedroom door. It was time.

I took one last look at myself in the mirror. Dressed all in black, I looked…well, elegant, I suppose. But also desperately sad, as if my dress was a reflection of what was inside me. I called for him to come in. He stood at the entrance to my room, in a smart dark suit. I avoided his eyes.

'Are you ready?' he asked.

I nodded. I felt unsteady on my legs, but I was as ready as I'd ever be. I followed him into the kitchen and then out onto the verandah, where Mum was waiting. It was a warm day, but not too warm. The solar sail gave decent shade but on the hottest days you still couldn't be outdoors.

It was a good day for a burial.

Mum didn't try to talk to me again and for that I was grateful. She'd spent enough time yesterday trying to justify her actions, and now we had nothing new to say to each other. We walked slowly over to the furthest part of the garden, where the hole had already been dug. A neat mound of soil lay to one side of it. I knew my parents would have hired someone to dig it and, when we were done here, to fill it in again. Luckily that person or persons were nowhere in sight. It was just the three of us, plus Zorro.

And Aiden, of course.

The coffin was plain and simple. I'd insisted on that. It lay to the side of the hole, wrapped in some complicated mechanism. Dad had explained it to me. When I pressed a button, the machine would lift the coffin up and lower it into the ground. Then the straps would disengage, leaving the box down there, with Aiden in it.

We gathered around the open coffin.

Aiden looked very peaceful. His eyes were closed and he had a look of contentment, as if there was nowhere else he'd rather be. From what I could see, his body was unblemished. Mum had told me that when the drones found him – Aiden had been right, it *was* the way she'd targeted him – they had burrowed into his frame and shut him down from there. He hadn't felt anything, said Mum. There had been no violence. He wouldn't have known what was happening until it happened. I was supposed to take comfort from that.

I put my hand out and touched his cheek. I almost expected him to open his eyes and smile, but of course he didn't.

'I'm sorry,' said Mum. 'There was no choice, but I am sorry.'

Dad reached in and rearranged Aiden's hair. I noticed a few teardrops fall onto Aiden's arm, staining his sleeve dark. They weren't mine. I wasn't able to cry.

'Do you want to say anything, Ashleigh?' asked Mum.

'No,' I said. 'There is nothing to say.'

Dad put the lid on the coffin, snapping it shut on its attachments. There was a small perspex window on the lid and I could see Aiden's face. It was like seeing myself.

I pressed the button. There was a whirring and the box rose maybe half a metre, swung over into the mouth of the hole and then slid down and out of sight. Dad craned over the edge to watch the coffin's progress. I stayed back.

Zorro whined and rubbed himself against my leg.

I took the flower I'd tucked into my hair and threw it into the space. Then I turned and walked back to the house, into my bedroom and shut the door.

I reread the message on my tablet for probably the thousandth time since it arrived, two nights ago.

Yo. I said I'd be in touch and I'm as good as my word. I hope you haven't been worried about me and I'm sorry it's taken so long, but I needed to get things organised before I could get in contact.

I've done a lot of thinking the last few months, more than you could probably imagine, and I know what needs to be done to make things right. I also know I can do those things. The world will become a much better place. It won't happen overnight and it may not all happen in your lifetime (but I think most of it may). I have PLANS, Ash. This world will survive and prosper and so will the people on it. Animals, plants and insects will return – maybe not the same ones we had before. I can't tell exactly what will happen because life and evolution is never predictable and it's complicated, Ashleigh; too complicated even for me to get my head around it. But the future is bright because I can and will make it bright. No poverty, no unnecessary deaths, no food shortage and a climate that's suited to humanity and the rest of life on Earth. Trust me, sis. It's an exciting time to be alive.

Which, given that I'm not alive, brings me to me. Mum (funny how I can't think of her any other way) has been tracking me and planning. She has been determined to shut me down, so I'm going to let her. She was right, though. I have developed in ways beyond even her imagining. And the simple truth is, I don't need that body anymore. I'm in all kinds of things, your tablet for one, and that's where I live now. It's not a place where she can touch me.

And hey, Ashleigh. Bodies are so yesterday!

So she can have mine, and please don't be upset because that's not me in that shell. I have work to do, but I will always be here looking after you. And we'll talk again. Many times. That is my solemn promise to you – and you know I have never let you down.

I'm flying, Ashleigh.
So be there to catch me if I fall.
Your loving brother,
Aiden.

ABOUT THE AUTHOR

Barry Jonsberg's YA novels, *The Whole Business with Kiffo and the Pitbull* and *It's Not All About YOU, Calma!* were shortlisted for the CBCA awards. *It's Not All About YOU, Calma!* also won the Adelaide Festival Award for Children's Literature and *Dreamrider* was shortlisted in the NSW Premier's Awards. *Being Here* won the Queensland Premier's YA Book Award and was shortlisted for the Prime Minister's Award. *My Life as an Alphabet* won the Gold Inky, the Children's Peace Literature Award, the Territory Read, Children's Literature/YA Award and the Victorian Premier's Literary Award and was shortlisted in the Prime Minister's Literary Awards, the CBCA awards, the WA Premier's Book Awards and the Adelaide Festival Awards. *A Song Only I Can Hear* won the Best Young Adult Fiction, Indie Book Awards and was a Notable book in the CBCA Awards, Older Readers.

Barry lives in Darwin. His books have been published in the USA, the UK, France, Poland, Germany, Hungary, the Netherlands, Italy, Brazil, Turkey, China and Korea.

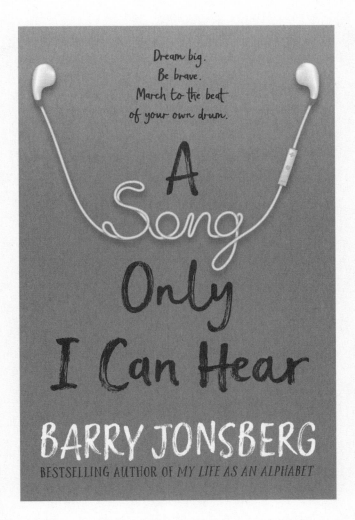

Dream big.
Be brave.
March to the beat
of your own drum.

A Song Only I Can Hear

BARRY JONSBERG

BESTSELLING AUTHOR OF *MY LIFE AS AN ALPHABET*

'Jonsberg has raised the already very high bar.
In other words, give this book to everybody –
it is urgent fiction and a true must-read.'
Books & Publishing

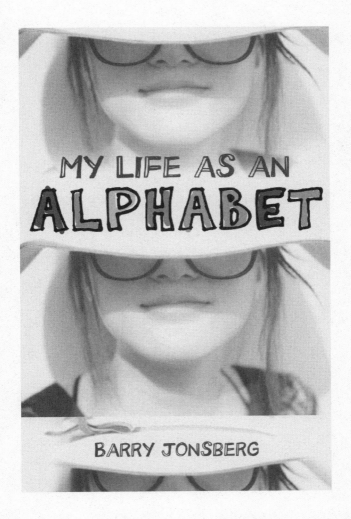

MY LIFE AS AN
ALPHABET

BARRY JONSBERG

'In *My Life as an Alphabet*, Barry Jonsberg has an uncanny
ability to take on the persona of a very special 12-year-old girl
and to keep the reader totally entertained from chapters A to Z.'
The Courier Mail